THE BIG BET

The Four Racketeers

Owen B. Greenwald

EPIC
Press

The Four Racketeers
The Big Bet: Book #1

Written by Owen B. Greenwald

Copyright © 2016 by Abdo Consulting Group, Inc.

Published by EPIC Press™
PO Box 398166
Minneapolis, MN 55439

Cover design by Candice Keimig
Images for cover art obtained from iStockPhoto.com
Edited by Ryan Hume

LIBRARY OF CONGRESS CATALOGING-IN-PUBLICATION DATA

Greenwald, Owen B.
The four racketeers / Owen B. Greenwald.
p. cm. — (The big bet ; #1)
Summary: Jason Jorgensen is the most unique guy among the rest of his class—because the club he leads is a front for a group of scam artists. Spurred on by a new
addition to the team, Jason tackles his biggest con yet: rigging a local poker game.
But this isn't like their high school plots—this is real and very dangerous.
ISBN 978-1-68076-183-2 (hardcover)
1. Swindlers and swindling—Fiction. 2. Deception—Fiction. 3. Young adult
fiction. I. Title.
[Fic]—dc23
2015949053

EPICPRESS.COM

For Roger Ganas, the first person who told me I could write (specifically, "If you don't become a writer when you grow up, I'll kick your ass"), and by extension, The Peninsula School, for ten magical years of childhood

PROLOGUE

IT'S HARD STAYING COOL WHEN YOU'RE BEING threatened by six men with guns.

But at least it wasn't seven, so it could've been harder.

The men were heavyset, with the look of people who enjoyed hitting things for pleasure as well as business. One had forgotten to turn his safety off, but I didn't feel like reminding him.

Richard, the only one not tied to a chair or holding a gun, was seconds away from full-on maniacal laughter. I couldn't blame him for that, or even for holding us at gunpoint in his basement—we kinda deserved it.

But I *could* still blame him for being a smug little asshole. That was all him.

"Clock's ticking," he said, with the most punchable smirk I'd ever seen. "And if time runs out before you tell me where the money is, Thomas is gonna plant a bullet in your brain."

I couldn't tell which of our captors was Thomas— they all looked the same to me. But it didn't really *matter* which of them would be shooting us.

"Thomas loves sharing, see," Richard continued. "He just put a nifty bullet into his pistol and he wants to share it with your gray matter. But if you decide to give us the money, he *might* get so distracted he forgets the whole thing."

Was it just me, or was Richard somewhat obsessed with this Thomas guy?

"Real tragic figure, Thomas. He distracts so easily. And his gifts are always *so* misunderstood."

It wasn't just me.

You might be wondering how somebody as talented—and devilishly handsome—as I found himself in such a compromising situation. Not gonna lie, it takes talent. Fortunately—or unfortunately, in this instance—I've got talent to spare.

I'm Jason, by the way. Jason Jorgensen, if you *must* know—yes, the alliteration's a crime against humanity. Now imagine having to live with it for seventeen years. I suppose you could call me the mastermind. Or boss, or leader, or head honcho—I'm not exactly picky. Deference is deference.

My position *technically* means I'm to blame for this whole mess, but that only matters if I can't also get us *out* of it.

"Wait," I said before Richard could start talking again. I couldn't hear much more about Thomas before my brain started punching the inside of my skull. "Let's talk things over."

"Let's tell them where the money is," said Z immediately. And for good reason. Whenever a plan goes wrong, Z *always* gets screwed over hardest. It's past coincidence at this point, more like a talent—but, you know, the opposite.

You're probably wondering, "What kind of a

name is Z?" We don't know either, but it's the best we've got. Z knows *everyone*. Even you, probably.

Now you're thinking, "But I don't know anyone named Z." That's the thing—Z never introduces himself the same way twice. I've walked down a street and (all in the same stroll) seen a vendor greet him as Zachary, a policeman call him Zeb, and a cabbie shout, "Zaim!" through a thick beard as they hugged so enthusiastically, you'd swear they were long-lost brothers. So rather than trying to remember who knows Z by what name, we keep things simple—Z it is.

There are two other things you should know about Z. First, he's in it for the money. Second, he cares *way* too much about his hair.

The tall girl to my right couldn't help herself. "Might be the right move. Even *I* couldn't take them all before they shot Z."

"What? Why me?"

"C'mon, bruh. You know it'd be you."

Z hung his head. "Yeah."

That's Kira, and she loves fighting to the point

where she's seriously considering trying to punch out six armed thugs. Other hobbies include hacking computers, ignoring speed limits, and listening to ear-bustingly loud music. Two of these hobbies are pretty handy. The other one's just annoying. Kira lives for adrenaline, and I'm pretty sure that's what keeps her on board. That, and tormenting Z.

"Can we focus?" said Addie. "Men? Guns? Remember?"

Addie likes stealing things, and lucky for her, she's incredibly good at it. She's quiet, unobtrusive, and never stays in your memory long enough to remember exactly what she looked like—if you see her at all, that is. I don't understand how she does it, because she should be turning heads wherever she goes. I may be biased—I have a thing for her. I wasn't sure if she felt the same, but I wouldn't be surprised. I'm quite the catch.

Addie's got her own problems that only money can solve. Before we turned her talents towards more . . . noble pursuits, she was a petty thief. Now she operates on a much grander scale.

Kira gave a purposefully visible yawn. "I've seen tougher." Far as I knew, that wasn't true. But it *was* Kira—I could believe she'd fought something scarier than six gunmen and never mentioned it. Who knows what she got into in her free time?

"You kids are crazy!" yelled one of the gunmen. I decided this one was Thomas. "Tell me where it is or I'll shoot you! You've got five seconds!"

Richard wagged his index finger like the gunman was a naughty child, and he fell silent almost instantly.

I let my amusement tug the corners of my lips upward. "You got us. We're all irredeemably crazy. Why else would we try swindling you?"

Ah, banter. Nothing distracts and confuses your victims—or possible executioners—like witty repartee. It's an essential part of any group dynamic.

Not everyone appreciates wit like I do. Lucas is a perfect example—he's got the comedic inclinations of a wolf spider. Actually, wolf spiders aren't big, mean, or angry enough to accurately describe that egomaniacal mountain of a man who thinks his intellect even *approaches* my own.

You'll have to excuse me. I ramble when I get worked up, and nothing works me up like the old man. I've heard absent fathers lead to broken homes, but in my case, that would've been an improvement. I have a few scattered happy memories of him, all hazy half-recollections from before I turned three. After that, I was nothing to him but a disappointment. No idea what he expected of a three-year-old—maybe a small business with steadily rising profit margins, ready to go public by the time I hit the ancient age of four. *That* might've impressed him.

Okay. I may have some father issues.

But it *does* give me a nice visualization tool for planning. I just imagine our mark is Lucas Jorgensen, and a hundred ways to wreck their lives and take their money come pouring in. My talents are never *un*impressive, but they work best when properly coaxed.

"But not as crazy as you guys," I said, as friendly as I could be under the circumstances. "Working for a guy who doesn't appreciate you. From where I'm standing—"

"Shut it," warned Richard.

"Look, dude." I turned to address him. "Not my fault you value Thomas over the rest of your help. He's obviously something special. But can't you throw the others a bone too? They deserve to feel like they matter."

Psychology has recognized the effects of in-groups and outgroups on the human brain since before we came up with the terminology to describe them. There were two distinct groups right now, which had unfortunate implications for the way Richard's thugs were probably viewing us. By "othering" Thomas, I was muddying the waters, loosening the bonds of the group, maybe even creating a third. These guys were *just* dumb enough to fall for it. The next step would be making *us* look like members of their in-group, but Richard wasn't about to let me.

"It's like you four don't realize that every time you say something that *isn't* where the money is, you get closer to us shooting you dead."

Oooh, very nice. Stressing *you four*, and *us shooting you dead*. Reinforcing the preexisting groups.

Richard had noticed what I was doing and taken steps to counter it. That rat bastard.

"Boss?" asked Addie conversationally. "Point of inquiry?

"Go ahead."

"If he can't find the money without us, and he kills us because we didn't tell him . . . how will he find it?"

"Wonderful question," I replied. "So much for *that* cunning plan."

"The *plan*," said Richard through gritted teeth, "is to kill you one at a time until one of you booger-eating brats wises up and squeals. Thomas is a patient fellow. He doesn't have to kill you all at once."

I sighed theatrically. "Alright, alright. I'll cut you some slack out of respect for Thomas, who is undoubtedly a paragon of humanity. You wanna know where the money is? I'll show you."

My friends looked unsure if I was serious or setting up a punchline. Well, if they were hoping for laughs, they'd be disappointed.

"Look, you guys," I said in my best contrite voice

(I don't do contrite very well), "The plan's pretty shot up at this point."

Kira and Richard both winced.

"Pardon the pun," I added quickly. "Point is, money's no use to us if we're all dead. Might as well tell them *before* one of us dies, rather than after."

I could *feel* Addie's gaze burning into my temple without looking at her. I knew how much she needed that money. "I couldn't live with myself if something happened to one of you because of me," I said. "I'll make Richard let you go before I tell him anything."

Richard laughed. "What a swell guy you are, Jace. Offering to stay behind and lie once your friends are safely away."

"I don't want anything to happen to *me* either," I pointed out. "I'll come with you, show you exactly where we hid it. Then you can kill me if I'm lying."

Richard tried to contort his face into the expression of a man who *wasn't* thinking he'd kill me either way, and failed miserably.

Great.

"Alright, here's how it'll work," said Richard suddenly. "We'll keep your little friends at a safe house. You come with me. If you try stalling me, or gosnitch to the police, I make a phone call and Thomas gets to be generous with *all* of you. You show me the cash and we can forget this ever happened. Understood?"

"That sounds a lot like *not* letting them go," I pointed out, trying not to look at the others. I didn't need any distractions right now.

Richard snapped his fingers and his goons all cocked their guns simultaneously. You had to appreciate the work that must've gone into that—a few hours' practice, at least. Probably more, if I'd accurately measured their collective intellect. But despite its over-choreographed nature, it was an effective reminder of my actual bargaining power.

" . . . But that's fine, I guess."

Richard smiled indulgently as one of his thugs undid my bonds. I stood up and looked at my friends, whose stares held identical levels of contempt. They knew—like me—that Richard had no intention of letting them go. But the look of naked betrayal on Addie's face sank under my skin and settled into my bones—even though I *knew* it was affected. Addie's face only showed more than a hint of emotion if she let it.

But the pain was real, even if the expression wasn't. She'd been counting on that money.

"Addie," I said quietly. "Before I met you, I had trouble coming out of my shell. See, I was content to stick with petty crimes, silly stuff. You helped me see the bigger picture, that there were a hundred eighty-four ways to apply myself. Lucas told me there were ten paths to self-actualization . . . guess I chose the eleventh avenue. Friendship."

A bunch of sentimental crap, but I promise you, I said it for good reason. Reasons are like suits—you should always have a good one on hand.

Richard, still smiling, motioned at one of the gunmen. "Take him to the car. I'll give these fellas their orders and then be right with you."

My captor, who resembled a rhinoceros who'd learned to stand on two legs, grabbed me roughly by the shoulder and dragged me towards the door. My friends' angry stares followed us out.

I know you'd love to hear what happened next, but it just occurred to me that I never answered your first question, how things got to this point. It's an extraordinary tale full of extraordinary people, and well worth hearing. Besides, you can appreciate *this* situation much better once you know how we got here.

It all began with the club I started—the Club for Perfect Cleanliness.

ONE

THE CLUB FOR PERFECT CLEANLINESS WAS PROBABLY the biggest joke in school. Until sophomore year, it had escaped notice among the other extraneous clubs at Van Buren High, but someone had eventually examined the list with more than cursory detail and word had spread.

That was alright, though. Laughs I could take, as long as I was clean.

Two years later, though, the joke had worn thin. Part of it was how the CPC's members conducted themselves—heads held high, without a trace of shame on our immaculately washed faces.

So we numbered only three, including me, but

not everyone really *appreciates* cleanliness—the thrill of washing your hair, scrubbing between your toes, or plucking your eyebrows. I assure you, you're incomplete without it.

We didn't let just anyone in, either. In the early days, there'd been a flurry of fake applications from people hoping to get in on the "joke". We'd explained that perfect cleanliness was serious business—with an item-by-item cleaning ritual as long as their arm to illustrate our point.

They never came back.

Our itinerary was technically public record (today, we'd officially led a discussion on proper tooth-brushing stroke technique), but nobody ever showed up, except our mandatory faculty sponsor/supervisor. And *he* . . . well, suffice to say we were left unsupervised.

But you can cover only so much business every lunch period, so we often continued our discussions after school, usually piled into Kira's car on our way to Scoops for some afternoon ice cream. This lovely Wednesday was no exception.

"Nicky can host Blackjack," said Z. "He just texted me."

One more task I could cross off. If I could distribute the pre-calc answer sheets and flesh out our fake school lunch distributor's website tonight, my to-do list would be in decent shape.

"Awesome," I said. "Heard anything about Jordan Bissel-Prynn?"

"I did," said Kira from the driver's seat. "She's not backing down. Anonymous notes aren't gonna phase her."

Isn't it *annoying* when people don't react how they should?

"Fire up the rumor mill," I said. "Start with everything we got from Sarah O'Connor—this'll be much easier with a wedge between her and Jordan."

Alright, I wasn't completely honest before. The CPC *is* a real club, but its members couldn't care less about cleanliness—except Z, who, as I mentioned, *loves* his hair. We just needed a place to meet without fear of interruption. We even designed the name to deflect interest. If I could redo things, I'd make it *less* stupid so it wasn't as memorable, but I'm not *always* perfect—just mostly. Sure, membership ruined our chance at popularity—again, except Z, who has more friends than Mark Zuckerberg—but it's a small sacrifice for guaranteed privacy.

What are we, then, if not hygiene enthusiasts? That's a tough question—our activities include everything from bribery to theft, and no Van Buren-ite—student or teacher—is safe.

The shortest answer's probably: We're con artists.

The club was my idea, of course. Kira does it for the thrill, Z for the money, but for me it's about pushing myself, finding a challenge.

And lately, there hadn't been one. Bribing teachers? Defrauding Mr. Appargus, our principal? Running card tournaments? We were capable of more.

"Will do," said Z. "My treat today, FYI."

He was smirking in an ask-me-why sort of way, so I gave a loud sigh and said, slowly and deliberately, "What's the occ—"

"Oh, it was great," Z said at once. "I'm in

Brooklyn, hanging out with Brian, and we're having a blast in the truck. And he—"

"You forgot to explain who Brian is," said Kira loudly, as she does every time Z tells a story and forgets we don't know everyone involved—which is every story he tells, because even phone books have *nothing* on Z.

"You should at least know *Brian*. Remember the Bratwurst truck always hanging around Harwick? We got sausage that one time and I told the owner to say hi to y'all?"

Kira sucked in air through her teeth and blew a raspberry.

"You *totally* remember. You just don't wanna admit it. What'd you think 'the truck' meant?"

"Figured you'd explain later," shrugged Kira.

She started backing into a parking space. Z looked put out that she'd derailed his story so fast, but that didn't stop him. He was used to it.

"So I'm hanging with Brian in the truck, eating my sausage, helping him with the lunchtime rush. Then he mentions this new truck keeps taking his spot." He paused. "Uh, if y'all didn't know, that's way uncool in food-truck land."

"Everyone knows *that*," said Kira, interrupting again. Not being the center of attention made her antsy. I, not being an expert on food-truck etiquette, appreciated the clarification, but I was courteous enough to stay quiet.

The car stopped and Kira twisted the ignition key. We emerged from the car, Z still trying to finish his story.

"This truck's been splitting his customers, taking his real estate, calling cops on him for no reason. What's a friend to do?" But his question went unanswered, because at that moment came a loud, desperate shout.

"Someone stop her!"

Three men—two thickset, one small and slender—were running full-tilt up the sidewalk toward us, weaving through the press of pedestrians with limited success. And desperately trying to keep ahead of them, ducking past grabbing hands and slow-moving bodies . . .

I'm above high school romance, but if there's one girl who could change that, it'd be Addie Bristol. She's in my history class, two seats to my left and one row towards the front, and she's . . . well, *captivating*.

Funny thing is, I didn't even notice she existed until, like, halfway through last semester. But one day, she turned around to check the clock and that's when I saw it—the secret hiding behind those bright green eyes. She's been on my mind ever since. You have no idea how *rare* it is to find someone with a secret. Usually, I can figure people out—not Addie. And she has this quiet smile, like she *knows* I can't. Like she's challenging me.

I don't back down from challenges.

So when I saw Addie Bristol running down that sidewalk, raven hair fluttering behind her, small hands clutching something unidentifiable to her chest, my mind was bright with possibilities. Now was my chance to uncover Addie Bristol's secret. And if getting her out of trouble was an opportunity to

break the ice in suitably dramatic fashion, well . . .
I'd be dumb to turn it down.

I turned to my partners in crime, unspoken question hanging in the air between us.

"No," said Z.

"*Hell,* no," said Kira.

"But—"

"Not our problem," said Z. "The club's gotta stay out of the spotlight. If we get caught . . . "

He was right, was the most infuriating part.

I was so close to asking as a friend, and owing them a favor. But then the questions would come— *Why do you care?*—and I didn't want them thinking I had a . . . well, a *thing* for Addie. I'd never hear the end of it.

Kira saw my hesitation and started laughing. "Right. I almost forgot."

She eyed me like I was a worm on a hook—or rather, a worm that had just fallen *off* the hook. That look never means anything good, and that goes double for Kira.

"Z, Jason here's got a little crush."

I choked on my own spit.

"Cute, huh?" she continued, obviously enjoying herself. "So let's play wingman for him. What are friends for, right?"

Now Z was laughing too. I stared at them in disbelief. "How'd you—"

"Everyone knows," laughed Kira. "You admit it?"

"I didn't say that."

Kira crossed her arms. "If you don't admit it, there's no reason to help."

Addie passed us, maintaining her breakneck speed. The men weren't far behind.

I gritted my teeth. "Fine. I admit it."

"Great!" Kira bubbled. "Z, you in?"

"I'm in . . . but you owe me one."

They looked at me expectantly—laugh and tease as they might, they knew our plan could only come from me.

"Z, in?" I asked, meaning "Do you have an in?" The three pursuers passed us, still calling for help. I heard sirens in the distance.

Z gave me a thumbs-up. He *always* had an in.

Kira started the engine and pulled back into the road a little too quickly, provoking loud honks from other drivers but somehow avoiding a fender-bender.

I haven't decided if Kira's an exceptionally skilled driver or just inordinately lucky. She drives like a menace, but that just makes it more impressive that I can't remember her ever actually *crashing*.

"Earbuds," I said, and we all slipped them in. I pulled out my phone and set up a three-way call. This way, we could keep each other updated, and—more importantly—I could share my beautiful voice with Kira and Z wherever they went.

"I have a plan," I half lied. "Z, run interference. Kira, let me out a block up and prepare to extract."

Kira smiled her best mayhem smile. "You got it."

We skidded to a halt. Z was out before the car stopped moving, running towards Addie's pursuers, who were again behind us.

"Carlos!" he shouted, embracing one of the thick-set men. "How've you been?"

That's all I heard—Kira was already pulling away—but it didn't look like Carlos was willing to stop and chat. Ah, well. I hadn't needed *much* of a delay. *Work with what you're given,* said Lucas's voice in my head. I tried to shut him out.

For whatever reason—probably because he tried to mold me into a predatory businessman from age two—a troubling chunk of my thoughts have Lucas's voice—mostly nuggets of advice he drilled into me.

"Here," I said, and Kira hit the brakes again. I burst out of the car and charged across the sidewalk into the doorframe of Captain Jack's Bar and Grill.

My plan, you ask? As Addie ran by, I'd guide her into the restaurant, which I knew had both a back entrance into an alleyway and a restroom. We'd run through making a big scene, then once we were in the back and out of sight, I'd send her into the restroom and stay behind to tell her pursuers she'd run out the door.

Not my best (what if the restroom was occupied?), but I was pressed for time.

I expected Addie to run by maybe five seconds after I hid myself. I counted fifteen, then stuck my head out.

She was gone.

I scanned the sidewalk again, but there was no sign—no, there were the men, pointing angrily *above* the sidewalk. I followed their fingers with my eyes and saw her, balanced on a storefront's awning . . . until she vaulted herself onto the roof.

It was clear that whatever I thought I'd known about Addie Bristol was woefully incomplete. Shouting angrily, the men on the ground split up, presumably to await her descent in likely areas. They'd probably wanted to follow her, but—like me—couldn't figure out how *she*'d made the climb.

I didn't move. Instead, I began to model Addie's decision-making process.

As I did, I reached for my phone, which was still connected to the others. "Z, who's Carlos?"

"Extra security at the gold exchange down the way," replied Z. "I think Addie took something from it."

"Yes, I can put *that* much together," I said dryly. "Alright. Z, move towards Second and Bowery. I'm outside Captain Jack's."

She'd never *struck* me as a thief—but then, she'd make a pretty bad thief if she had. Which she obviously wasn't, judging by the way she'd made use of Z's distraction to scale the wall. *And* she'd known, whether through instinct or analysis, that she had to get off the street and stay unpredictable to have a chance of escaping—with almost *no* time to make that decision. She was a smart one. Maybe even almost as smart as me.

I won't say I fell in love as I put this together, because I didn't, but I *might've*, if I'd been the weepy, romantic type. I certainly didn't regret helping her—stealing isn't enough to unsettle *me*. Everyone steals from everyone else. Some are more blatant than others, and those are the ones you can trust to make their intentions obvious. That's another Lucas-ism.

But obvious intentions don't make for obvious actions, and I needed to predict her next move to catch up. No *way* was I climbing that awning. So I determined what *I'd* do in her position. And then I stayed exactly where I was.

Sure enough, about a minute later, Addie

reappeared on the rooftop and started climbing down the way she'd come, landing catlike on the awning with a soft thump that made a group of tourists jump in alarm. None of them seemed to know what to do.

She slid gracefully over the edge and hung there for a couple seconds, then dropped the remaining feet to the pavement. As the pedestrians decided whether to ignore or apprehend her, she slid in among them.

I blinked. I'd been *looking right at her*, and I could still barely keep track of her. She moved with the crowd like a fish through the current, utterly at home amid the rush of bodies—which, though they'd been watching her only seconds ago, now treated her like just another face in the crowd. I followed, keeping her firmly in my sights.

"Jason?" That was Kira, coming in clear through the earbud. "Boys in blue coming your way. You still on Fifth?"

I sped up and grabbed the phone. "Yup. Thanks for the warning. Z, I might need a crowd in a hurry. You on Second and and Bowery yet?"

"Yep. This where you want the crowd?"

"Gold star," I said, then slid the phone back into my pocket as I caught up with Addie. I brushed her arm deliberately, and she glanced towards me.

"Cops are coming," I said in a low voice. Confusion blossomed like an orchid across her face as she recognized me, and I realized that might've been the first thing I'd ever said to her. I wished I'd picked my words better—"Cops are coming" wasn't snappy *or* clever. Not up to my usual standards at all.

"Safer on Second," I said, continuing to disappoint my internal repartee-judges. "C'mon."

Addie didn't break stride, and her green eyes narrowed in suspicion. "Where did *you* come from?"

"Heaven. Can't you tell?"

There, that was better. A solid eight from the judges.

She rolled her eyes. "Jason, right?"

Ouch. "The one and only. Really, though, we should turn left here . . . "

"And I should trust you because . . . "

"Over there!"

Before I'd registered the shout, Addie was already on the move, zigzagging through the crowd away from the policemen pushing their way towards us. I followed as best I could, and noticed with relief that she was making the left. Things go much smoother when people follow my advice.

"Kira, little more warning next time."

"Doing my best, boss," said Kira. "You want an extraction?"

"Gimmie a sec," I said, breaking into a run as the crowd thinned. "Z, we're almost on top of you."

"Gonna buy me dinner first?"

"Not. The. Time."

"Right. We're ready. They think it's a viral stunt."

"Copy," I said, somewhat amazed he'd pulled it off. Who else but Z could've gathered a crowd on such short notice? He's got a special way with people I can only envy—my intelligence tends to intimidate them.

I glanced behind me. The cops were closing the distance with long strides. The lead cop had shoulders the size of hams, and the look on his mustached, sweating, tomato-red face promised some "accidental" bruising if he caught us. I gritted my teeth, summoned my reserves, and drew even with Addie, reminding myself that a well-exercised mind doesn't translate to a well-exercised body, and that the latter can be more useful than I expect.

"Aim . . . for the crowd," I said between breaths.

"Crazy?" panted Addie, not taking the time for superfluous words.

"They'll let us . . . through," I explained, hoping I was right. I caught Z's eye, and then we plunged into the sea of pedestrians. They parted before us like we were Moses himself split into two. I felt them close ranks behind me, becoming an impassable wall of flesh. Addie looked at me with sudden respect, and I almost punched the air in delight.

"Kira," I said into my phone. "Heading your way . . . down Second. Extraction . . . *now.*"

"Alright, but I'm starting the meter as soon as you get in."

I was surrounded by wannabe comedians.

"Cops're asking for backup," said Z into my ear.

"They're pissed about the road block. Jason, get off Bowery and turn on Bleecker."

"Turn on Bleecker," I said to Addie, and she nodded once.

"Motherfucker," Kira swore. "I'm way outta position. Mmkay. Meet me at Elizabeth before the situation gets any—"

"Don't say it," said Z.

"—bleaker."

I ignored them and kept running.

"So . . . you do this . . . often?" I asked.

That got a small smile. "Not telling. You?"

"More . . . than you'd think."

"Crap," said Z. "Bleecker's one-way back towards the cops. You want Houston, one down."

"Works for me," said Kira over loud honking. "Bleecker was giving me trouble anyway."

"Left on Elizabeth," I said to Addie. She nodded again. Neither of us said anything more, conserving our breath for the run.

We sat the moment we reached Houston, gasping for air. Addie's hand relaxed around the object it was holding—a jewelry box. Likely earrings, from the shape. She saw me looking and tucked it behind her leg, shooting me a hard look. I sat there and tried to look trustworthy.

"Kira, where are you?" I said into my phone, partly just to break the awkwardness.

"Late," she offered.

"That's not an answer—"

"Houston, we have a problem," said Z, and I could hear his smirk at one-upping Kira's joke through the phone. "I've been tagging along with Jones, and they figured out where you are from asking bystanders. They're sending a car down Elizabeth in both directions."

As he said it, I heard sirens approaching. "Kira," I said, "again, *where are you?*"

A squad car pulled around the corner a couple blocks down, and my heart dropped into my stomach. They'd found us first. It drew steadily nearer, not moving particularly quickly. Why would it? We weren't going anywhere, not fast enough to outrun a car.

Suddenly, Addie's face was in front of mine, blocking the approaching car from view. "Can't let them see you," she muttered. "Then they can't identify you later . . ."

"There's not gonna be a 'later'," I admitted. "Sorry. I think we screwed this one up. Thanks, though."

I couldn't see the car anymore, but the sirens were building in volume, gradually applying more and more pressure to my poor, beleaguered morale. But there was something else beneath the wailing, growing louder.

The harsh roar of a revving engine.

I whipped my head out from behind Addie's body just in time to see a familiar red Civic swerve around the squad car, practically brushing the bumper.

The cops surged after it, but had to brake to avoid crashing as the Civic skidded to a halt in front of us, leaving tire marks on the pavement. The windows were open and through them thumped a heavy dubstep beat, which overpowered even the now-earsplitting sirens.

"Ready for prom, you crazy kids?" bellowed Kira, somehow making herself heard over the din.

She threw open the passenger door and I jumped into the seat. Addie dove through the open window into the back, and Kira put the pedal to the floor. With a squealing of tires, we accelerated down Houston, police escort not far behind.

"What took you?" I asked in mock anger, but Kira just flipped me off.

One second, the road ahead was open. The next, another police car had turned the corner right into our path. Without missing a beat, Kira spun the steering wheel, swerving even as the second car slammed on its brakes. The maneuver took us onto the sidewalk with an awful crunch and a jolt as our tires met the curb.

Kira laughed triumphantly. She took the turn faster than turns should *ever* be taken, then hit the brakes, bringing the car to a shuddering halt in the middle of the street.

"The hell are you—"

"Check this shit out," said Kira, shifting into reverse. "And hold onto your nutsacks."

She looked over her right shoulder and accelerated wildly, steering the Civic into a flawless parallel parking job, sandwiched between two other cars bumper-to-bumper. It couldn't have taken more than few seconds.

No sooner had she killed the ignition than two police cars, sirens blaring, pulled around the corner and sped past us.

I let out a long breath and sagged into my seat. Addie's eyes were like silver dollars as she stared at Kira in unabashed amazement. "That was *really cool*," she said. "Why didn't I know you could do that?"

Kira turned around in her seat, wearing an exhilarated smile, and extended a hand, palm up. "You forgot to tip me."

TWO

"**N**OT TO SOUND UNGRATEFUL, BUT . . . WHAT'S going on?" asked Addie.

We'd replaced the license plates (my idea, FYI, to have extras ready. It never hurts to be prepared) and switched on Kira's cop tracker app. Our car's description was certainly circulating by now, probably our faces too. Before we could get moving, though, we had to wait for Z . . . and figure out what to do with Addie.

You know what we did with her—it comes with starting in the middle. But *we* didn't know yet, and there's this whole narrative . . . just play along for a bit.

"Those aren't ordinary earrings," I said, keeping my face as straight as possible. "They fell to Earth in a mysterious black box made of an unknown material. They're engraved with an alien message, and what little we've translated suggests they outline the secret of eternal life. We were tasked by the Government with retrieving them safely. We're part of a secret organization."

Addie looked at me skeptically.

"But we're not here for *them*," I continued. "Actually, they can only be touched by the line of the Chosen, which is its own separate thing. You're this generation's Chosen, so we're oath-bound to protect you at all costs . . . and find you a suitable mate to continue the Chosen line until the apocalypse begins."

Some experts on lying recommend taking refuge in audacity—telling fibs so outlandish, people will conclude you *must* be telling the truth. This was . . . a step beyond that. I could tell Addie hadn't believed a word after, "It's simple."

"Really," I said. "Ever heard of the Guillari alien affair?"

"No."

"Exactly. That's how good we are at what we do."

Addie rolled her eyes. "Kira. What's going on?"

Kira turned around. "I could tell you," she said in a bad Russian accent. "But then I'd have to kill you."

Addie was losing patience, so I seized the moment. "Hypothetically, *if* we brought her on board, we could tell her everything, right?"

This hadn't been in the plan, but there's no reason I couldn't *pretend* . . .

"So *that's* your angle," said Addie, like the world had gone back to making sense.

Kira's forehead creased with doubt. "I dunno . . . "

"She's good," I said. "You weren't watching her, but we could use her skills."

Studies indicate that when trying to convince someone to do something, it's best to have one voice encouraging them, and another goading them by doubting their abilities. Kira hasn't read those studies (I'm not sure she reads), but she's naturally contrary, so I usually use her as the goad.

"The CPC doesn't admit just anyone," said Kira. "She's gotta be really *special.*"

Addie looked incredulous. "Is this about that stupid club?"

"The CPC is anything but stupid," I said in a hushed whisper. "Together, we accomplish things you've never dreamed of. Remember Roger Klein's prom-posal?"

Addie smiled broadly, remembering. "That was *you?*"

Roger Klein was Van Buren's quarterback, and he believed it made him king of the school. Come prom, he'd started pressuring the head cheerleader, Anne Doolie, to go with him. Anne refused multiple times, but he'd persisted, getting a little angrier each time. Kira hadn't appreciated that.

I'll never forget the room-shaking laughter as he sprinted to the front of assembly in a full-body dog suit—and neither will he, with the whole school reminding him daily. Needless to say, he'd gone to prom dateless.

"All us," I said proudly.

Kira started the car. "Look who's here."

She jabbed her thumb out the window. Z was on his way across the street, looking worried.

"Thank God y'all are okay," he said. "What a mess. They're gonna have descriptions circulating . . . pics of the car and its plates . . . this was pretty bad."

He threw open the passenger door in disgust. "Guess we got lucky."

"I'll get into the system and delete them as soon as I get home," Kira promised.

"They'll be waiting there," I pointed out. "They can trace who owns the car with the old plates. Your parents're probably gonna hear their car was used in a robbery, so you should start planning what to say. But you can stay at my place until the heat's off and use my Wi-Fi to change the records."

"So the CPC is a front," said Addie. "That . . . makes sense, actually."

Z jumped at the sound. I don't think he'd noticed Addie yet. "Course not," he said immediately. "What gave you that idea?"

"*We* did," replied Kira. "Don't worry, Addie's cool. Right, Addie?"

Addie looked hesitant.

"C'moooon," said Kira. "We need another chick anyway. And did I mention the perks? All that sweet, sweet cash, for starters."

The hesitant look vanished. "You guys make money?"

"Make, not so much," I admitted. "But it comes our way." I indicated the jewelry box she was still clutching. "You'd be familiar enough with that."

Addie shrugged. "I guess denial's pointless."

"Hey, no judgment here," said Z. "That's kinda what we're about."

" . . . Then I'm in."

"Yes!" Kira pumped her fist.

"Wait a second," said Z. I shot him a look of pure poison and he backpedaled immediately. "Not saying she can't, it's just . . . what can she *do*, exactly?"

I rose to the defense of our newest member. "She—"

"Stealth," said Addie before I could continue. Her voice was quiet but self-assured. "Acrobatics, lock-picking, disguise, lie-reading. Is that enough, or should I continue?"

Her eyes bored into Z's, daring him to challenge her again. Instead, he found something incredibly interesting about his cup holder.

"And *she* can speak for herself, thank you."

I felt my cheeks heating up.

Kira chuckled. "I like you."

"I'm in, then?" said Addie, with only a trace of smugness.

"Long as you swear to keep our secrets, yeah," said Kira. "That's rule one. What happens within the CPC, stays within the CPC. Unless we're scouting a new recruit."

Addie smiled. "I'm no stranger to secrets."

She was doing it again—practically *dangling* her secrets over my head with that smile. But I could be patient. Now that she was on the team, I could pick Addie Bristol apart at my leisure.

In the most romantic way possible, that is.

"That's good," said Z. He'd picked up on the smile too. "Just remember, there's no secrets between each other."

Addie's smile wavered slightly.

"Not relating to club business, anyway," Z clarified, and Addie nodded, satisfied. "That's our third rule—"

"—That only I can break," I said.

"—That *not even Jason* can break."

Whatever. It was a stupid rule. Some plans work better when the people involved don't have all the information. Whatever Z insisted, I wasn't gonna handicap myself because the club's rules said to.

"Rule four," I said, changing the subject. "Z's least favorite rule. Cash from a job, if applicable, is split evenly among those involved."

The rules are serious stuff, the backbone of the CPC. Each was crafted and codified with the utmost deference and care at our very first meeting.

"Rule five," I said with a smirk, "is that during meetings, I'm to be addressed as 'sir,' or 'my liege.'"

"Rule five-and-a-half," said Z quickly, "is we can disregard rule five at any time. There *is* no rule number six, and rule seven is, don't feed the gremlins after midnight."

We'd gotten bored five minutes in and started messing around.

"All on pain of death, mind," said Kira, winking.

"Ignore rules five through seven, got it. But was there a number two?"

"It's the same as number one," I said. "Don't ask."

Kira, who watched *Fight Club* at least once a month, had threatened to quit unless we stuck a repetition of rule one into the list as rule two. She'd lobbied for the wording, "The first rule of the CPC is, don't talk about the CPC," but we'd talked her down.

"There's a couple unofficial rules," said Z. "Stuff we never wrote down, but kinda developed. Like, if someone in the club helps you out and it ain't club business, you owe them. And unless someone offers to pay, we play credit card roulette when we go out to eat. That's it, though."

Addie frowned. "Credit card roulette?"

"It's dead simple," said Kira. "Everyone puts in their card and whichever one gets picked gets charged."

"And you go out . . . often?"

"Oh yeah," said Z. "Pretty much every day."

Addie hesitated, and that's when I noticed that she was still clutching that jewelry box like she was worried about someone taking it from her. She hadn't stolen it for fun—she needed it. The idea of going out to eat every day—and then *gambling with the check*—might be repugnant to her.

None of this showed on her face, of course. I was surprised she hid it so well, at the time, but I learned pretty quickly that Addie doesn't show a single emotion she doesn't deliberately let through her mask. But I wasn't reading her face, just her circumstances, and those gave me the hints I needed to make sense of her behavior.

I noted *risk-averse* under *Addie* in my mental list of peoples' traits, and said, "It's mostly a formality. With the kind of cash the CPC brings in, meals are loose change. Think of it as a business expense."

I didn't explicitly *say* it'd be a net profit for the same reason I didn't offer to pay her meals—it'd only draw attention to her discomfort, and I knew she wouldn't appreciate that. But she was smart enough to read between the lines, do a quick cost/benefit analysis, and see where the balance lay.

"Then, sure," said Addie. "Let's do this."

There was no stopping the wide smile that spread over my face. If she'd gotten *this* close and then turned us down over *credit card roulette* of all things, I never would've forgiven Z for bringing it up.

"Welcome to the team," I said. It sounded dumber out loud.

Kira turned around in her seat, punched my shoulder lightly as if to say, "Go get her, stud," then—thankfully—looked back at the road.

THREE

"**I** CALL THIS MEETING OF THE CLUB FOR PERFECT Cleanliness to order!"

Three days later, none of us had gotten any official-sounding knocks on our doors. I'd expected an investigation, even sketched out plans to circumvent it, but there was nothing. That seemed off to me, regardless of any hacking Kira had managed. But she said she'd "handled it," and I didn't inquire further.

As usual for our meetings, Room 206 was dimly lit—mood lighting's important, after all. The four of us sat around a table, which had at its center a small, glass fishbowl. Within the fishbowl, swimming contentedly above a scattering of multicolored rocks, was a single goldfish, barely visible in the dim light.

Needless to say, the teachers can't know the truth about the CPC. However, all Van Buren High clubs require a faculty sponsor's supervision. This presented a problem, and surprisingly, it was Kira who solved it. She sliced into the school's admin account and created an entirely new faculty profile, Mr. Algernon Gildfin (Algie for short), to sign off as our sponsor. And that's why CPC meetings are officially presided over by an aging goldfish.

Addie sat across from me, looking right through me with those bright green eyes, two gleaming points in a face otherwise lost in shadows. She'd picked up all the traditions without any trouble, even the ones we'd made up on the spot to test how far she'd play along. Thankfully, Kira and Z had been quiet about the whole . . . *crush* . . . thing, but I didn't trust their self-restraint to hold out. Gildfin was also saying nothing, but that was less surprising.

But you aren't interested in boring romantic crap.

You're here for the drama and the handsome, witty protagonist who keeps it coming.

I stood dramatically. "Ladies and gentlemen—"

"Gentle*man*," corrected Kira, then looked towards Addie for an air-five. She got one.

I continued, undeterred. "For too long have we been content to lie happily before the fireplace of our successes. The world turns, opportunities rise and fall, but we shut our windows and curl up by the warm and comforting. A scam here, a caper there, but where's it all *going*? Do we not want more? Do we not *deserve* more?"

Z looked like he was about to answer, so I swept on briskly. "That was a rhetorical question. And here's another—Do you agree? Of course you do. Kira, raising the stakes means raising the challenge. Z, raising the stakes means a bigger payoff for you. Addie, as the newest member of the group, you'll pretend to go along with what the senior members unanimously agree on because you don't want to make waves or be seen as a problem member."

There was silence as the others tried and failed to disagree with my analysis.

"Well, when you put it that way," said Kira, cracking her knuckles. "Yeah. No objections here."

"One second," said Addie. "I'm *sure* Jason won't disappoint, but I'd like to hear exactly what he's thinking before I sign on."

So much for advance commitment and the pressure of consistency.

"And I," said Z, "wanna know where I get screwed over."

"Nowhere," I said, a little too quickly. "I never *plan* things to go wrong—"

"—I just always end up in detention, or bitten by a dog, or falling into a sewage tank. And don't even get me *started* on the Jackie Ernwall caper—"

"I'm putting *myself* in danger this time," I reassured him. "This goes wrong, I take the fall."

"If *what* goes wrong?"

"Poker."

Ever since the meeting before we'd recruited Addie, I'd been trying to come up with something *big.* Inspiration had finally struck during a James Bond movie marathon. I'd been thinking about how suave and charming James Bond was, and how easy it would've been for *him* to sweep Addie Bristol off her feet, and *that* made me think I could be a pretty good secret agent. I was already handsome and clever, and what he'd been doing—playing poker—I could *already* do, if I wanted.

And then, because it'd take skill and practice *on top of* genius to win a *real* high-stakes game, I'd embroidered the plan somewhat.

"More specifically," I elaborated, "cheating at it."

"Right," said Z, "because—"

"To the tune of at least a million dollars."

There. *Now* I had everyone's attention. Particularly Addie's—she was fixing me with a very intent gaze, and the secret-smile was hovering about her face. Even Professor Gildfin looked attentive as he flapped around his bubble of glass, though that could've been my imagination.

"I've talked with the Blackjack crew," I explained. "Finally found one for whom it runs in the family.

His dad frequents a secret, semi-regular, high-stakes poker game right here in the city. We rig it and walk out rich."

"What if they come after us?" asked Addie. "If I was a regular player and some newbie won big, my first thought would be that he cheated."

"We'll have to make the cheating really, *really* subtle—"

"Doesn't matter, if their hypothesis isn't evidence-based," said Addie.

"Point," I said. Addie grinned and Kira shot her an astonished look, as if getting me to concede an argument is a rare, freak event. Which it is. But Addie had used the word *hypothesis*—someone in this group *finally* spoke my language. I have no problem conceding to *correct* arguments. Not my fault Z and Kira never have any.

"Alright, they won't trust a *total* stranger. But what if someone they know already vouched for him?"

Addie's brow creased in thought. "But who'd vouch for *you*?"

I glanced over at Z. "Z's probably got a few friends in the game who'd vouch for *him*."

"No way," said Z. "You promised. This time, you're doing it."

"I know, I know," I said. "That wasn't serious—we need to actually *win* the poker game, not just gain admittance. I wouldn't trust you to win a game of Connect Four."

"Challenge accepted."

"Connect Four tournament, Z's place!" shouted Kira, desperately trying to stay in the conversation. She never felt at home during the planning segments.

"Kira," I said, and she perked up immediately. "I'll need you to investigate this poker game. They've gotta have a listserv, an IRC, a livejournal . . . something. Find it and crack it open."

"I'll ask around too," said Z. "Like you said, I probably know some people."

We all looked at Addie.

"And *I*," she declared, "have to work on my APUSH paper. Good luck with your stuff, though." She smiled. "Got to stick with our strengths, right?"

As much as I'd hoped to use the search as an excuse to hang out with her, I had to concede she had nothing to offer this part of the operation. And it was probably better that way—even welcome distractions are unwelcome sometimes.

As it was, I hung out at Kira's place all night, sharing what Z had learned as she followed electronic trails to their digital dead ends, cursing up a storm whenever she did so. Somewhere between the fifth and sixth pot of coffee, we hit pay dirt.

"Alright, everyone," I said the next day, tossing a stack of printouts into the center of the table. "Check this guy out."

"Richard Trieze," read Addie. "Thirty-four, CEO of Imperial Tech, lives in Washington DC, graduated from Tufts with—why am I reading this again?"

"He's our man," I explained. "Kira found him."

"He's going to vouch for you?"

"Nope," I said with my best shit-eating grin. "Someone's already vouched for *him*."

"Flying in from out of town," explained Kira, with a grin every bit as wide, but more predatory.

"He's played poker online for a while with this dude Brad, one of the other players, and they're about to meet face to face for the first time. Turns out this group doesn't let in new blood, but they're making an exception for Richard here."

"Or rather," I finished triumphantly, "for me. Meet the new Richard—smarter, funnier, and sexier."

Richard, according to his picture on Imperial Tech's website, was short and weasel-like, with limp black curls and a small mouth. And that was the picture he'd *chosen*. Truth be told, I was doubting my ability to play the role convincingly. How did the appearance-challenged denizens of the world *behave*?

Z frowned, but Addie was tapping her chin thoughtfully. "It could work. The truth will come out eventually, but we'll be gone by then. . . . Or they'll have already done a thorough background check, know what Richard's supposed to look like, and call bullshit the moment you walk in."

"It's a possibility." The information age made capers *hard*. But not as hard as they'd be without a master hacker on the team.

It wouldn't help if they'd already looked, but . . . "Kira, can you get into Imperial Tech's site and swap his picture out for mine? Maybe disguise the changes on their end?"

"Well, you can use cookies to—" Kira caught herself. "Yep. No prob."

"Do it ASAP," I said, and she mock-saluted.

"How do we deal with Richard?" asked Z.

"Working on it," I said. "But c'mon, the guy's a *tech CEO*. How hard could it be?"

Some CEOs are ruthless cutthroats, hardened by years climbing the corporate ladder. Not so with tech CEOs—they're usually spoiled rich kids who got lucky with their first startup. Soft as tomatoes, the lot of them. That was another reason Richard made a perfect target. He wouldn't even know what hit him.

"His friend knows him too well," I said. "We'll have to deal with him too . . . No, Kira, stop smiling."

Kira pouted. "I never get to hit stuff."

"Get over it. I'm not changing the plan so you can get your kicks. It's already perfect."

And it was. Sure, some details needed ironing,

some risks were unavoidable—as always. But if con artistry was easy, *everyone* would do it. And I was *proud* of what I'd put together. Danny Ocean himself couldn't have done better.

Neither could Lucas.

FOUR

A HALF HOUR BEFORE RICHARD'S PLANE WAS SCHEDULED to land at JFK, we were already in position. Addie was keeping tabs on Richard's plane and Z was waiting for his cue, which left Kira and me on the curb outside baggage claim, watching the drivers suffer and making small talk.

"Seriously, bruh, grab life by the balls. She's *totes* into you."

I hate small talk.

"Can we just focus?" I asked, knowing it was pointless.

"I can focus," said Kira, shrugging and flipping her blond hair behind her back. "I'm worried about *you* zoning out and screwing something up, so it's my duty to get all that steamy sexual tension out in the open."

A buzzing sound. Kira reached into her pocket. "It's Addie. Plane's landed."

"I'd estimate we have ten minutes, maybe fifteen. Tell me when he reaches baggage claim." A thought hit me. "Crap. We don't know if he checked a bag."

I could hear Lucas berating me for my mistake, and shut him down, *hard*. I didn't need that right now. It wasn't even that big a slip-up. But the plan had several specific beats, and the presence or absence of an extra bag could throw in unwanted wrinkles. And I *really* should've realized.

"See? You slipped up. Steamy. Sexual. Tension."

I sighed. "One day, you're gonna tease me in front of her, and then our lives will be ruined."

"*Our* lives? Just yours, boss."

"Trust me, I'd make sure yours was too."

"Alright, alright, I'll stop joshing you. Fingers crossed," said Kira, suddenly serious. "I'm just happy for you, is all."

"Really." My tone was as dry as the concrete we stood on.

"Well, I also like seeing you discomforted."

"You wanna see me discomforted, just wait for the stats quiz this Thursday," I said, electing to change the subject. Kira was like a charging bull—impossible to stop but easy to divert. "Haven't studied, and the way things are looking, I'm not gonna have time."

"You and me both, bruh." Kira shook her head sadly. "I don't even *remember* what a P-value is. Or that sixty-four, ninety-three, something bullshit—"

"It's sixty-eight, ninety-five, ninety-nine, and it's the percentage of the population that, on average, falls within various standard deviations of the mean," I recited. "C'mon, that's day one stuff."

"Missed fifth period, day one, remember?" said Kira, grinning. "I was in Appargus's office for punching out some dudebro."

"It's like you just put your entire academic history into context," I said. "Okay, lemme refresh you. Do you know what a population is? In terms of stats, I mean."

The resulting pop quiz revealed several barn-sized gaps in Kira's stats knowledge, and I resolved to talk with Ms. Petunia vis-à-vis Kira's final grade. I just couldn't let Kira find out—she didn't like having her weaknesses pointed out or covered for. Kira didn't like remembering she *had* weaknesses, and those she acknowledged, she took a stubborn pride in.

We were discussing conditional probability when Kira's phone vibrated again.

"He'll be out in maybe a minute. Doesn't look like he packed a bag."

"Keep your eyes peeled," I said, dialing Z. "Yo. Party's starting soon."

"Hey, Jace. Doing my best here," said Z. "We're pretty far, so maybe delay the party a bit? I wanna see you guys." Which meant, *Delay him if you can, and stay on the line.*

"Don't worry," I said, though my fingers were tapping a railing nervously. "Just get here when you can."

Addie came out the doors first, and quickly strode over. "He's right behind me," she muttered.

"Yeah, I got cups," said Z in my ear, carrying on a mundane side conversation with nobody to keep up appearances.

A few seconds later, I got my first look at the man whose identity I'd be borrowing. He was even more unimpressive in person, blinking passionlessly as he scanned the road for taxis. And there was no shortage of taxis.

I turned away from the others, trying to look like just a guy on the phone. "Z?"

"We're one short," said Z. "Getting closer. Everything cool on your end?"

One *what* short? Airline? Car-length? Loop section? "Could you be—"

"Daddy!" That was Addie's voice.

I whirled around to see Addie's arms wrapped around Richard's back. He spun around, surprised, and Addie dropped back, stammering apologies. "You looked *just* like him, sorry," I heard her say. Behind her back, a brown leather wallet vanished into the back pocket of her jeans.

"That's—don't worry, I understand," Richard

said, eyes darting back towards the road. "Well, I've gotta get to my hotel . . . you know."

"Sorry," said Addie again, and disengaged, joining the crowd again.

And still, Z was nowhere to be seen.

"Kira," I said, pointing at an empty taxi that had just pulled over. Richard had noticed it, was trying to make eye contact with the driver. But Kira was already there, climbing in and smiling amiably at the cabbie. The cab pulled away and Richard shook his head in frustration, muttering something about teenagers.

I was ready to do the same thing if necessary, but I was the only other person free. If a *third* cab pulled up before Z arrived . . .

Timing. This is why timing is important. But this particular bit of timing was like throwing a dart blindfolded and ringing someone's doorbell from across the street.

Another taxi pulled up, and I prepared to race Richard to it, but then I saw Z in the passenger seat and felt a surge of relief. Just as well, too—this time, Richard practically *pounced* on it.

The driver was Z's friend, of course, though I couldn't remember his name. Z was accompanying him for the day, learning the ins and outs of the profession. The man didn't understand why Z would *ever* consider that career, but was happy to do his friend a favor.

He didn't know Z knew I'd bribed him to be here at this time, for this traveler. And yes, I'd bribed him *before* Z asked to drive around in his taxi, not after. I'm not an *amateur,* I *understand* that people have a harder time noticing causation backwards. I've done the research.

Z told me he'd call back, then hung up and hopped out of the taxi with a helpful, easygoing grin, then hefted Richard's carry-on. I drifted closer, trying to hear their conversation.

My phone dinged. It was Addie.

On our way.

I caught Z's eye and made a *hurry up* gesture.

Z shoved the carry-on into the trunk, and smoothly slipped something into an outer pocket.

The airport's sliding doors opened and Addie walked through, followed by two airport security officers. Her eyes swept the crowd, then she pointed confidently at Richard's taxi.

Z, meanwhile, was chatting with another recent flight survivor, probably another friend. They always were.

"Back in the car, Zane!" said the driver. "We're on the clock!"

"Excuse me, sir," said one of the officers, striding up to the window. "We'd like to talk to you."

The man's brow wrinkled in confusion. "Something wrong?"

"Maybe, maybe not," said the officer. "We've been told—"

"You're not gonna arrest us, are you?" asked Z, wide-eyed, all innocence.

The officer ignored him. "—told that airport patrons heard your passenger discussing the sale of illegal drugs on the phone, which he managed to sneak through security."

"What?" said Richard sharply. "That's ridiculous!"

"Mister, we have what's called probable cause to search your luggage," said the second officer, who was sporting a trim black mustache. "We don't find anything, you're free to go."

Richard shrugged in defeat, eyes narrowed in suspicion. I could almost hear him thinking, *What are the odds that something's gonna be in there? Zero, right? But if this is a setup . . .*

The driver popped the trunk.

I watched as the officers opened the suitcase, but not intently. Richard didn't need a reason to remember my face.

"Well, well, well," said mustache-officer. "What have we here?" Dangling from his fingers was a small plastic bag filled with white powder.

Richard paled. "It's not mine," he said immediately.

"This your luggage?" asked mustache-officer, lifting the bag.

"Yes, but I didn't pack that."

The other officer sighed. "Heard it before."

Richard's face reddened and he plunged his hands into his pockets angrily. I don't know what he was planning—Did he want to bribe them? Show his ID? Call someone?—but his expression transformed into one of pure horror when he realized they were empty.

"You don't understand," he pleaded. "I'm being set up. My wallet and phone are missing, they planted drugs on my bag—"

"The cops'll sort things out at the station, mister," said mustache-officer, not buying a word.

Richard buried his head in his hands. "I don't believe this."

I didn't hear anything else. I was already walking away, into the thick of the crowd. The next stage of the plan required timing just as delicate as this. Maybe more so.

I dialed Kira.

"Kira here, what's swingin'?"

"Hey. You found Roxy's address, right?"

Roxy was the linchpin of the poker game, and

perhaps the only person everyone there trusted—or so we'd picked up from their listserv. She organized the games, vetted the guests, and took the role of dealer at the games themselves. If anyone had already researched Richard, it was her.

For all his aesthetic faults, Richard was a smart guy. You don't become CEO of a large company without *some* wiles. His arrest wouldn't keep him out of commission for long, and his first priority—even while detained—would be to notify his friend Brad, or possibly Roxy. Maybe both.

Which meant we needed to get to them first.

"Yeah," said Kira. "And a whole lot more, too. One thirty-three Rutland Road. Also, her name isn't really Roxy. It's Annette Nast. She hid her tracks pretty well—masked her IP and everything—but you can't hide from me. I deserve a raise, b-t-dubs."

"I'll mention it next shareholder meeting." I rolled my eyes. "Z's headed to Brad's, so it'll just be us three. See you in a bit."

"K, see you in a bit," Kira repeated back. "Oh, and Jason?"

"Yeah?"

"If you guys wanna stop somewhere and bone or something, that's cool. Just lemme know you'll be late."

"*Goodbye*, Kira." *As if* I'd jeopardize the plan like that. Well . . . maybe I would. Too bad it was all hypothetical—

"Anything else before we leave?" said a voice unexpectedly from behind me.

I jumped, and then my brain remembered the voice was Addie's. "You're too good at that," I admonished.

"Please. It'll save your life someday."

"No doubt," I said clumsily, trying to keep my rapier wit on point. "Everything went without a hitch, by the way."

"I figured," she said. "It's only been a few days, but I've picked up that your plans tend to work."

My cheeks were doing their best hotplate impression again. I *had* to get that under control. "I'd say they work every time, about . . . say, ninety percent of the time."

Addie looked like she was about to say something, but swallowed it.

"Also, I saw you pocket the wallet, but Richard said his cellphone was missing too."

"Got both," said Addie, waggling a Nexus Six in my face with a triumphant flourish. "I don't leave jobs half done."

"But I only saw you grab the wallet," I protested.

"If you could see everything I did, I wouldn't be too helpful, would I?"

The secret-smile was back. I let the matter drop and waved over a taxi. A real one this time.

FIVE

"ONE THIRTY-SEVEN RUTLAND ROAD," I SAID TO OUR driver, who waved accommodatingly and punched the address into his GPS with robotic precision.

You never give the driver the actual address, just in case he's called to testify later. Though I'd had Addie locate and block the taxi's security camera first thing, there was no reason not to be safe.

The best plans are simple, and this one was no exception. If Annette didn't answer when we knocked, we'd ransack the house. If she *did*, we'd wait until she left and *then* ransack the house. Addie would spot and deactivate the security systems, I'd rummage through the rooms, and Kira would get into her computer, all in pursuit of the same goal—leverage. Blackmail was the only way I could think to get Annette on our side, and we *needed* Annette on our side. The others would be watching me like hawks, but not *her*. They trusted her.

And if we couldn't find any leverage, I'd think of something else. But people like Annette always have *something.*

"GPS says we have eighteen minutes," Addie reported.

"Plenty of time."

"Not nearly," she said regretfully.

My pulse quickened. She couldn't mean—but unless I was imagining that look of longing . . .

"Too bad—this was the perfect time to get our history homework out of the way."

"Oh, right. History." Definitely imagined it. I backpedaled harder than a hipster on a multispeed. "We probably should've warned you—CPC business eats your free time."

"Really?" she said impishly. "I hadn't noticed."

"It's not usually this bad." I grinned ruefully. "This is the biggest thing we've ever done."

There was a silence, too long a silence before I realized what I *should* have said. *L'esprit d'escalier,* it's called in France, literally *staircase wit*—thinking of the perfect response too late.

Was it too late? The conversation's parameters hadn't changed . . . But every second of silence deepened that gap irrevocably. So I forced myself to say it anyway, before it became even *more* awkward, pretending the idea'd just come to me and *hadn't* been stewing in my brain while I considered saying it—

" . . . But my history grade *is* kinda suffering, now you mention it," I said. Not technically true, but it was for a good cause. "Wanna meet up after this and do the homework then?"

She smiled, and this time, there was no secret behind it. "Yes, let's. Your place alright? My place is kind of . . . awkward."

A shadow passed briefly over her face and I didn't press further, even though I *really, really* wanted to.

"My place is pretty bad too, honestly, but sure. I'll have to go back either way, so you might as well come too."

"Yeah? What's so bad about *your* house?"

"For starters, it's not really a *house* . . . more a mansion. Big, fancy . . . really *garish*, you know? Like Lucas—that's my . . . you know—had it built to rub his dick in his neighbors' faces."

She laughed at that. "So you live in a mansion. Your life sounds *really* hard. I bet you're in danger of being crushed to death by falling piles of money, too."

"I didn't mean—"

"No, by all means. I'm sure it *sucks* when Scrooge McDuck shows up at your family reunions. Do you know what *we* could do with mansion-money?" Addie's tone was lighthearted, but I could tell I'd touched on something sensitive. Time to steer the conversation elsewhere.

"Maybe it's not *all* bad. Having a big house helps me keep as far away from Lucas as possible."

"That bad, huh?"

A dozen competing anecdotes sprang to mind amidst a flurry of descriptive adjectives, all swirling together in my mind to outline the hulking shape of Lucas Jorgensen. The bright light shining through the windows dimmed slightly, like a cloud had passed across the sun, but the sky was a brilliant, unbroken blue.

I chose one. "One Christmas, I wouldn't go to bed because I wanted to wait for Santa, so he sat me down at the dinner table and explained that Santa wasn't real, and that I had to 'divest myself of childish games if I wanted to succeed in life'."

"Ouch."

"I was *five*."

"That's harsh." Addie looked like she was trying to hold back more laughter. Not that I blamed her—it *was* pretty funny, in hindsight. Cartoonish, almost. But it was just one of the ways that *cockroach* had shattered my childhood before I'd lived it.

"That's normal, for him. He said that dose of reality was the best Christmas present he had for me.

And he was right . . . but only because he didn't give me any others."

"My dad left when I was six," said Addie abruptly, like she was racing to get the words out before she could stop them, vomiting them into the taxi. "I don't really remember what he was like. But he can't have loved me very much, since he left."

"I'm sorr—"

"It's cool. I'm over it."

I could've one-upped her story, but I didn't.

"I wish *Lucas* would leave," I said at last, and Addie smiled, though it was small and bitter.

"I don't know," she said pensively. "I don't know what your dad's like . . . but Jason, growing up fatherless *hurt*. I felt his absence almost constantly, like my heart wasn't in my chest, always away on holiday. Birthdays were worse, or vacations, or the day before school started, but it never went away. I wouldn't want you to . . . "

But no more words came. It was like she'd formed a tight little ball of cold around her momentary vulnerability and walled it off before it snowballed into a battering ram of emotion.

Despite my interest, I let the conversation die. Partly because I know what it feels like, making that wall. Partly because if we kept talking, she might ask about Mom.

I don't like thinking about Mom.

Luckily, I was too distracted to dwell on those thoughts—I'd just stumbled on a gold mine of pieces to the puzzle that was Addie Bristol. Not enough for a complete picture—hints, no more—but a breakthrough just the same.

I was startled out of my reverie by my phone vibrating against my leg.

"Bad news," said Kira the moment I picked up. "Z's out of position."

"Hello to you too. What's that mean?"

"He just texted me. His friend the taxi dude wants to keep hanging, and he can't think of a way out."

"He can't say he has an appointment or something?"

Kira sighed. "He was pretty insistent. Said he

was sorry, and could probably get to Brad's in a few hours."

A few hours. Richard would *definitely* find a way to call him by then, if he hadn't already. "He knows this could ruin everything, right?"

"Bruh, I told him. But you know he gets weird about his friends."

"Do I need to yell at him?"

"He said you shouldn't call him. He's still in the cab, so you'd have to use code, and I don't think we have any for this situation."

"No, because this *wasn't supposed to happen*." But that was my fault—I should've planned for something like this, and a dozen other things besides. My brain was slipping into panic mode, so I closed my eyes for a second and shut it down. Panicking wouldn't solve anything. I needed my thoughts clear.

"I'm already here, b-t-dubs," said Kira. "Where are you guys? I'm growing old."

"Maybe a couple minutes out. Brad'll have to wait."

I felt a little sick saying that. Every second Brad

wasn't out of the picture was another second Richard could find a phone and sink the entire plan. But my current task had to take priority. I could think while we waited to see if Annette was in, but splitting my mental faculties was a recipe for disaster.

Two and a half minutes later, we pulled up to 137 Rutland Road, thanked the driver, and stepped out of the car into an idyllic suburban neighborhood. The sun formed dappled patterns through the large-leafed trees lining the street, and the houses were tall, thin, fashionably quaint affairs. The perfect place for a crime.

"Nice day for it," I said airily, and Addie smiled back, though I couldn't tell whether in agreement or amusement.

Kira was already lazily meandering towards us when we spotted her. We met her halfway, at the foot of the steps.

"Hey there, you fine, upstanding citizens," she said. "Up for a bit of crime-free gallivanting?"

I fist bumped her. "You know it."

Side by side, we ascended the brick steps to the

door. I grabbed the knocker and knocked three times. Then I jammed my hands into my pockets and pulled out a pencil.

"Footsteps," said Addie. I didn't hear anything, but before I could say that, the door opened.

Annette Nast was different than I'd imagined— younger, for one thing. She couldn't have been older than twenty-five. She was blond, blue-eyed, about Addie's height . . .

. . . About Addie's build . . .

"Hello?" she asked, looking confused—and under-standably so—to see three teenagers on her doorstep. Her accent was unmistakably German. Then again, with a name like Annette Nast, it would've been strange if it *weren't*.

I cleared my throat. "Pardon me, ma'am," I said smoothly. "My friends and I are playing a game, called 'Bigger or Better.' We started out with a paper clip, and we've been asking our neighbors if they'll trade us for something that's either *bigger* or *better*. Then we take that something to the next house and make the same offer. So far, we have"—I held up the pencil—"this pencil. Do you have anything you're willing to trade?"

For a moment, I didn't think she'd play along. Then—

"I'm sure I have something," she said, and went back into her house.

"Nice cover," said Addie, and I had to force a big dumb smile off my face. What was *wrong* with me?

Since Annette *was* home, the plan called for retreat. But there was an idea pressing against my brain, demanding to be indulged. Probably completely unfeasible, but here's the thing—it was too elegant to waste.

Of *course* I had to go for it.

I made the decision in less than a half-second. "Kira," I said under my breath. "Take her out."

Kira looked at me like I'd just sprouted antlers. "You—*what?*"

"Do it," I said with more confidence than my mental calculations warranted.

Kira froze until she could process that this was

actually happening, and then moved catlike into the house.

"Are you *insane*?" hissed Addie.

There was a thump from inside the house, followed by a muffled cry.

"Time will tell," I responded. "Haven't ruled it out, though."

I stepped inside and motioned for Addie to follow, ignoring the sounds of the continued struggle from the other room. Addie shut the door behind her.

We found Kira standing over an unconscious Annette, looking *very* pleased with herself. "That was fun," she remarked to nobody in particular.

"Now explain," said Addie. "Because I can only assume you've snapped."

"I came up with a better plan," I said. "You mentioned earlier that disguise is one of your strong points?"

"Sure."

"With a little work, you'd look *just* like Annette." The more I thought about this plan, the more I liked it—what it lacked in safety, it made up in pure audacity. "The eyes and hair are wrong, but those are changeable. Short heels would cover the height difference . . . You guys see it, right?"

"It's doable . . . " said Addie slowly, peering at Annette's unconscious body. "I've got some face putty at home for the cheeks and nose . . . My German's not the best, but it's workable . . . You're lucky I'm not darker."

Kira gave her a quizzical look.

"Spanish," explained Addie. "On my mom's side."

"No way."

"*Medio,*" she shrugged. "*Tengo piel blanco, pero mi madre es de España.*"

I couldn't *quite* parse that with my rudimentary Spanish, but Kira grinned. "Cool."

"I have to tell *everybody,*" Addie assured her. "I guess . . . I guess I got my looks from my dad."

I was pretty sure that had almost been something like, "I guess my looks are all my dad gave me."

"But if the other players all know and trust her, *someone*'s bound to notice—"

"You said you were good," said Kira. "Show us how good you can be."

"You can keep the lights dim," I assured her. "I bet they do that anyway. Dim lighting and illegal card games go together like bedbugs on a mattress."

"But personality-wise," Addie insisted.

"You've got a couple days to study," I said. "We'll need to keep her out of trouble—I'm thinking that's your job, Kira—and you can stay here and talk with her, pick up her habits. I trust you not to give anything away. Speaking of which, masks and gloves, everyone, from now on. We don't want her IDing us later."

Kira snorted. "Dude, she already saw us."

"But she wasn't actively trying to memorize our faces then. Let's not give her more than she already has, and hope that knock on the head fuzzed her short-term memory a bit."

Just mentioning that made Kira smile again.

Addie motioned me over as she was leaving to search for rope. "What if I'd said I wouldn't do it?"

"Huh?"

"Next time, before you give an order like that . . . ask me."

There was no anger in her voice, just reproach. I lowered my head. "Sorry," I muttered.

"I know you give the orders, but remember. We need to know what's going on. For the good of the plan as well as our peace of mind."

She was right, of course. But in this case . . . I tried to figure out if I'd had time to explain while Annette was still indoors. That was just a rationalization, though. I hadn't thought about it before giving Kira the order.

By the time Addie returned with rope, Kira had lowered the blinds. They began binding the still-limp Annette while I watched from her leather couch.

This part of the new plan had gone almost perfectly—time to turn my thoughts to Brad. Addie and Kira could hardly *un*-capture Annette if I left them alone for five minutes. Well, Kira could, but I trusted Addie to keep her in check.

He had to be dealt with *now*, before Richard got access to a phone. That ruled out my entire first wave of ideas. But restrictions breed creativity, and there were more solutions than what came to mind immediately. And sure enough . . .

"I just had another idea," I said, and explained the plan.

SIX

THE PLAN WAS SEMI-RELIANT ON KIRA REMEMBERING the full name of Richard's friend, Brad. I shouldn't have taken this step for granted, given that Kira's memory on the *best* of days is like a pack rat—it can hold onto one thing, but only if it puts something else down. When pressed, she said it was, "Brad Narwhal, or something." How sure was she? "Not very."

The only Brad in Richard's phone's contacts list was a "Brad Knowles". I decided that was close enough, and hit *call*.

He picked up on the third ring. "Hello?"

"I've landed," I said, trying to sound like

Richard—a little higher and nerdier than my own rich, robust voice. I didn't know whether my *words* were plausibly Richard's, but I was *hoping*. "Plans've changed."

"What's going on?" He sounded worried, but he hadn't said anything like, "You must be the man who stole Richard's phone," so I'd probably made the call in time—unless he was stringing me along . . .

"I'd rather explain in person," I said. "I'm staying at one thirty-three Rutland Road. Did you get that?"

" . . . Yes? Rich, you sound sick."

"Just a little harried. Trying to keep this call short. I'll explain later." Inspiration hit me and I added "I'm turning my phone off when I hang up, and you should too—they might be tracking it. How soon can you be here?"

"Tracking . . . Jesus, never mind. You want me to come to you? What about the Chelsea safe house?"

I was sure I'd misheard. "The what?"

"I said, what about the Chelsea safe house?"

No, I'd heard right the first time. But that didn't mean it made *sense*. Why did Brad need a safe house?

I looked at Addie helplessly. "Remind me where that is?"

"One eighty-four Eleventh Avenue." I could hear the exasperation in his voice.

"Um . . . no, not gonna work. Not there." It was the best excuse ever. I dare you to disagree.

"Rich, what's going on? You okay?"

"Just my past, coming back to haunt me," I improvised wildly. When in doubt, keep your statements vague, and the mark will imprint meaning onto them. Brad sounded pretty familiar with Richard, so he'd have no problem filling in the blanks. "Stuff I haven't told you . . . stuff you deserve to know."

"Alright. Be there in twenty. Even under the circumstances," a weak chuckle, "I'm excited to meet you face to face."

"Me too, Brad," I said. "See you soon."

I hung up, and then let out a long breath. Kira gave me a thumbs-up.

"Good job," said Addie. "Though you sounded a bit forced."

I had *not* sounded forced.

"Well, he bought it," I said defensively. "I think. We have twenty minutes."

I turned off Richard's phone in case Brad tried calling back.

Twenty minutes wasn't nearly enough time—turns out taking a prisoner is a complicated process. We had to find a proper room, secure it, remove any potential weapons, et cetera. Kira wanted to install a security camera, and spent five minutes searching Annette's house for one before she gave up. At T-minus-two, we gave up and stuck Addie (whose face was now swathed in one of Annette's shirts) in the room *with* her for now. Kira and I took our positions—her in a shadowy alcove off the front hallway, myself on the plush rug by the door. Unlike hers, my face was uncovered—*I* had to appear not-suspicious for a minute or so, and wrapping my head in cloth would definitely undermine that.

Four minutes later, the doorbell rang.

"Who is it?" I called, making my voice deeper.

This charade's lifespan was measured in seconds, but I'd keep it going as long as I could.

"It's Brad," came the reply.

"Brad who?"

"Brad Knowles," he said, wearily.

I opened the door.

Brad Knowles was short, portly, and bespectacled. He looked like a beleaguered accountant.

"You're not Richard," he said immediately.

I'd considered trying to pass myself off as Richard, gambling that they'd never actually met before. Good thing I hadn't.

"Mr. Trieze is waiting in the dining hall, Mr. Knowles," I said with a slight English inflection. "There are a great many things he wants to discuss. Please, follow me." With that, I withdrew further into the house. Brad hesitated a few seconds, but followed.

Halfway between the door and the kitchen, Kira hit him on the head with a paperweight.

He yelled in pain, but Kira's hand, wrapped in fabric, was already pressed against his mouth, and the noise barely traveled. Kira dropped the paperweight and snaked her other arm around his neck, slowly applying pressure. He grabbed at her arm, but her grip held easily—Kira's strong as hell.

I went to shut the door.

By the time I got back, Brad was supine on the ground, eyes closed. Kira was breathing a little hard, but she looked thoroughly elated.

"Nice work," I said. "Bind him and put him with Annette. And remember, when you talk to them, we're pretending to be employed by Richard. He's double-crossing Brad to cheat big time at the games, and we're bad at keeping that a secret."

We'd have to let Brad and Annette go eventually, and when we did, I wanted them busy chasing someone who *wasn't* us.

"Smart," said Kira.

"I know I am," I said smugly. "I'll make a checklist for you later, so you won't be deprived of my genius even once I've left. You know, keep the blinds down, the door locked, don't answer it—wait, unless it's Z. I might send him to keep you company."

Kira sighed theatrically. "I guess he's better than nothing."

She hoisted Brad by his armpits and half-pulled, half-carried him to the laundry room, where we'd decided to stow Annette. Putting our prisoners together was suboptimal, but we didn't have the resources to watch two different areas. My knuckles rapped the all-safe pattern by instinct, and Addie opened the door a crack.

"She's awake," she said, slightly muffled through the cloth. I pulled my own exposed face back from the doorway. "And not very happy. Bring him in."

She opened the door a little wider and Kira stepped into the opening with Brad's unconscious body in tow. I heard Annette exclaim in German.

"Start taking notes," I said.

Addie drew closer to me. "What if someone misses them before tomorrow night?"

I'd been thinking that too, but there are only so many restrictions you can accommodate before planning becomes impossible. "We'll worry about that when it happens," I said, knowing it was an obvious evasion. "For now, I need to brush up on my card counting, and you need to study Annette's speech patterns."

Airtight isn't a word I'd use to describe this new plan, but I couldn't help *wanting* to believe in it. I assured myself that it'd be fine—I'd play the game, win big, and we'd all walk away rich. But there's something I was forgetting, circling the edge of my memory . . .

"Alright," said Addie. "We're rain checking that study session, then."

Ah, yes. That was it.

Fuck.

SEVEN

THE MERCURY LOUNGE WAS A BIT OF A DIVE—UNIM-pressive gray exterior, tacky, slightly sticky interior. Just the place you *wouldn't* suspect was housing high-stakes poker games. But according to Z's friend, there was a basement room kept in much nicer condition exactly for that purpose. I was going there now, led by a maroon-vested bouncer who'd taken my precisely-worded request of *riskier entertainment* with a knowing smile.

Addie, looking every inch the mid-twenties German dealer, had naturally left early, carrying several marked decks. I was pretty confident nobody'd suspect any deck she supplied. Just in case that was wrong, Addie was armed with several excuses, two unmarked decks, and a host of backup plans.

Down the wooden steps we went, footsteps echoing hollowly in the narrow corridor. It grew darker and darker as we neared the bottom. On the last step, the bouncer stopped and waved me onward. "Have a good time, sir," he said, words crawling out of his mouth like they'd had to pry his lips open with a crowbar.

I pressed a fiver into his hand as I passed. Might as well make a good impression, just in case. It was too dark to tell, but I think he smiled.

The door ahead was also wood, but it was well-polished and intricately carved, standing out from the dinginess of the cellar. I took one last deep breath, dried my palms on my pants, and opened the door. No turning back now.

The room inside was small and intimate, with leather couches shoved up against red velvet walls. In the center of the room was a low wooden table and fourteen chairs. Above hung a marvelous crystal chandelier that gave the room an appropriately low, sinful lighting—so I'd guessed *that* right. On the whole, the setup and atmosphere weren't too far from the Blackjack games I'd been helping run since sophomore year, right down to the bar at the far end.

By the bar, a tall, broad-shouldered man with muscles like polished tree trunks (I *really* hoped he wasn't someone I'd be cleaning out) was chatting with a young blond woman who seemed oddly familiar. With a jolt of shock, I realized it was Addie. Her poise and demeanor were completely different (not to mention her hair). She hadn't lied—she *was* good at this.

Staring at Addie had kept me from noticing, but everyone was staring right back at *me*. All around the room, conversation had stopped at my entrance.

This was no good-natured Blackjack game. I was an outsider here—therefore, a threat. My throat was suddenly very dry, but I tried not to swallow. Swallowing was suspicious.

"And who are *you*?" asked a dark-haired man.

I adopted the thoughts and reactions of someone

who had every right to be here. "Richard Trieze. Pleased to meet you."

"Brad's friend," muttered a brunette in a navy-blue cocktail dress to her neighbor.

"Where's Brad?" asked an older gentleman, whose clothing was extremely fashionable . . . in the sixties.

"Family emergency," I said. "He sends his regrets."

Addie'd told me to *believe* every word I said. This seemed impossible since I was lying my ass off, but I was trying my best.

"He's on the level," Addie said in accented tones, quickly, before someone else challenged me. "Brad has explained the situation, and it is nothing to worry about." Her eyes flashed behind her contacts. "I want a pleasant visit for Richard, yes? Will that be a problem? Felton? Slater?"

"Not at all, Roxy," said the older gentleman, whom Addie'd addressed as Slater. He and a couple others still looked distrustful, but the rest seemed satisfied by her endorsement. Conversation started up again as people returned to their natural groupings.

"Thought you'd be older," remarked the dark-haired man, who was one of the suspicious ones. "Where'd Brad meet you, anyway?"

I gave him my best sinister smile. "In the world of online poker," I replied, "you can be any age you want. I've been playing the game for years."

There. Dodging the question with two technically true statements. Not my fault if he interpreted the word "game" differently than I'd intended.

The man was silent, but his gaze invited me to continue. I guess he actually wanted his question answered. Luckily, my arsenal of technically true statements was equal to the task.

"Brad was surprised, like you, when we met. But soon enough, I showed him what I was capable of. He was utterly shocked. A prodigy, you might call me." Might as well set up the expectation that I'd do well before I actually *started* to. That way, it would seem less like an excuse, and more like an explanation. "And I didn't catch your name, Mr . . . "

"Bryan," said the man. He still didn't look too enthused about me. Oh well, can't win 'em all.

"Lovely meeting you, Bryan," I said. "Brad's told me a lot about this scene."

Bryan narrowed his eyes suspiciously. "Like?"

Whoops.

"Like . . . how skilled you all are," I backpedaled. "DC doesn't put up a fight. I'm looking forward to a real challenge."

"You'll get one, Mr. Trieze," said Bryan, tone still cold. "You'll get one."

There's just no making friends with some people.

Actually, *everyone* I tried to engage was similarly guarded. By the time the last three gamblers had arrived, I'd managed to learn nothing but some names and that everyone resented my presence. Normally, I'm a pretty social guy, but I was relieved when the last player arrived and conversations died down.

I sat to the left of an old, gruff-looking gentleman named George, who I was hoping would be a mild-mannered, easily manipulated neighbor. He didn't seem actively hostile towards me, which was a plus, but I resolved to get a more detailed read as the night went on. Just an arm's length in front of me sat one hundred thousand dollars in casino chips, representing the game's entrance fee. Technically, I hadn't paid, but nobody needed to know that.

Addie stood at the other end of the table, riffling a deck. Her eyes passed over me without a glimmer of acknowledgement as she swept the lineup. She wasn't sitting, which meant thirteen people were gathered around the low wooden table. I couldn't tell whether that meant bad luck for me, or for them.

Slater tossed a black chip into the center, and I followed suit with everyone else. There were no small denominations in this game—ante started at $100, and climbed upwards in increments of that size or larger.

"Everyone in?" asked Camilla, a middle-aged lady who'd arrived after me.

"All in," confirmed Addie, and began to deal.

The game, as the expression goes, was afoot.

I looked at my cards. Nine of clubs and three of hearts. The flop had another nine, which gave me two of a kind. Not bad . . . but probably not round-winning in a thirteen-player game.

Betting began. Nobody committed too aggressively—all either seeing how the round played out or trying to lure the other players in. It was two hundred to stay in, and it'd be my turn to bid shortly. I took two black chips and tapped them on the table speculatively. Tap . . . tap . . . tap . . .

"Two hundred." George shook the chips in his hand before slapping them down.

I'd tapped my chips eight times. I tapped them twice more, then tossed them into the center.

I wasn't sure how Addie'd marked the deck—it was safer if I couldn't give anything away. But she'd assured me that if I communicated which card I wanted, she could find it and get it to the top without anyone noticing.

Everyone else watched the betting continue. I watched *her*. She was playing with the cards, shuffling them. Even watching for the sleight of hand, I couldn't see it.

The first round of betting finished. Six players had folded. Now for the fun part.

Addie leaned forward and—after "burning" the top card—flipped the nine of diamonds.

And betting began again among the seven remaining players.

I stared again at the cards in the middle. Nine of hearts. Jack of spades. Five of hearts. Nine of diamonds. If the next card flipped was a heart, that opened the possibility of a flush. If it was anything between a king and a seven, that opened the possibility of a straight. Both would beat my hand.

And all I really had was my nine. If another player had the fourth nine, they just needed higher than a three to beat me.

My *best* shot was to signal Addie for a three for the full house, but I *really* didn't want to be that lucky this early. That's the kind of luck that makes people suspicious, especially when the lucky man is a newcomer who keeps tapping the table weirdly.

I could always duck out later if the betting climbed too high. I shoved in $500 worth of chips and grit my teeth internally. *Ex*ternally, I wore a confident smile.

Three more people folded after seeing the nine.

I thought George was bluffing. He'd looked torn before matching the bet, like he was trying to decide between two *binary* choices, rather than calculating multiple odds at once. The other two, I was less sure about.

Addie burned two cards this time, and dealt the river. Ace of clubs. She *was* looking out for me. I resisted the urge to wink at her.

It fell to Alicia, a redhead with a perpetual scowl, to open the round. She tapped the table—a check.

I held my cards sideways, like I was about to fold. If George really *was* bluffing, seeing me on the verge of dropping out would entice him to bet—

"Four hundred," said George, pushing his chips into the center.

I tapped the table. Addie couldn't help me at this point, but I was trying to establish it as a habit.

"I raise," I said at last, trying to make it look like a tough decision.

I dropped $600 into the center. The fourth player called—not confident enough to raise. A good sign?

"I fold," said Alicia, and her scowl deepened.

I watched George carefully. On a logical level, he must've known folding would save him from losing money, as there were still two players he hadn't bullied out. On the other hand, human psychology just isn't good at cutting losses. "Throwing good money after bad, the expression goes." In psychology, "bad money" is called a "sunk cost." People *really* don't like backing away from already-committed resources.

But in the end, he folded. It was the rational, cool-headed choice, and I adjusted George's threat level accordingly.

My odds were good, I thought. "Three of a kind," I said, laying my hand on the table.

My last opponent's face fell. "Two pair," he said, flashing a five and an ace.

With a smile, I swept the pot into my pile. It was a good start to the night, but I wouldn't be satisfied until I had every last chip.

EIGHT

I LOST THE NEXT THREE ROUNDS—TWO FOLDS, ONE LOW hand. I probably could've spun the low hand into a win with Addie's help, but I wanted them to see me losing. Besides, the pot hadn't been big enough to matter.

Addie must've been fed up with me taking things slow, because in the fifth round, she handed me the ten of spades and the jack of hearts, and the flop consisted of the ten of diamonds and two other jacks.

Could've just been luck, but Bayesian probability suggested otherwise. The trick would be *not* signaling my fortune. Even a royal flush wouldn't mean much without a large pot . . .

"Four hundred," said Bryan. It was an aggressive starting bet, but he didn't betray a hint of doubt as he pushed his chips into the center.

"Fold," said Slater.

"Call," said the next player after some deliberation.

Nobody raised, including me, but nine people stayed in.

Addie burned a card, then flipped the turn. Six of diamonds.

And the betting began again.

"I call," I said when my turn came. I'd been tempted to raise, but it made sense to give the other players the opportunity to raise first so I could backraise later. My hunch ended up paying off, as Camilla raised to $800.

The next two players folded at that point, but the next one—Jordan, who was perhaps the youngest man there besides me—raised as well, to $1,000.

Again I had to fight to not look at Addie. Was *she* responsible for this?

I assumed Jordan was bluffing. If he had a good

hand, he'd want to bait other people into raising before committing. His current strategy seemed designed to push people out instead. But he'd picked a bad hand for it. This was the first major pot so far. It'd be hard to convince other players to walk away.

Betting passed to Bryan and he called. George took a long drink, then followed suit.

I paused.

If Jordan was bluffing, he'd either fold or raise again next round, which gave me another opportunity to backraise. Only this time, everyone would be even *more* invested in the pot.

Finally, I threw in another purple chip. "Call," I said again. Bryan was smiling at me—and not one of those affection-filled smiles, either. More like the smiles Lucas gives me.

So I pictured him sitting in Bryan's chair, and smiled right back.

The next round of betting began with six people still active. Addie dealt the river—seven of diamonds. I heard a sharp intake of breath from Felton. Not so good with discretion, then. I could work with that.

I called the bet when my turn came—this time at $1,300—and examined the board. Addie had set things up ingeniously. With the current setup—ten of diamonds, jack of spades, jack of diamonds, six of diamonds, seven of diamonds—all sorts of high-value hands were possible. Two diamonds made a flush, an eight and a nine made a straight, and a jack with a ten, six, or seven—what I had—made a full house, which lost only to four of a kind—currently impossible, since I had the fourth jack—and a straight flush, which was *possible*, but highly unlikely. I could rest easy knowing I had the hand, while several other players were no doubt convinced this was their moment.

True to form, Jordan raised again, to $2,500. However, I could see his nervousness. His plan wasn't working, but he'd committed too much to back out easily. I almost felt bad ripping him off. He was just a kid, really, even if he *was* rich enough to drop a hundred thousand on a game of poker.

Bryan called again, and George folded. I smiled, grabbed my yellow and two blacks . . . and picked up two more yellows. "Forty-five hundred," I said confidently. With any luck, my opponents would think I knew to fake confidence when I felt unsure, and would therefore conclude that I was bluffing, rather than modeling me as someone who knew that *everyone* knows to fake confidence when they're bluffing, and that it's therefore more misleading to be confident when you *are* confident, and unsure when you're unsure.

Levels of deception are hard—think *too* far ahead and you'll end up at the equivalent of a lower level and lose anyway. My play required some guesswork, but the principles behind it were sound—most people stay on level one unless they're actively trying to move beyond it.

Sure enough, Alicia called. Jordan, though, finally realized his strategy wasn't working, and folded.

It fell to Bryan to end the round. But if I'd read him correctly, he'd—

"Five thousand."

Yes. That.

"Six thousand," I countered.

Alicia had no choice but to call again, caught

between us as she was. It was clear from her ever-darkening expression that she'd be much happier with a smaller pot, but she wouldn't fold beneath the pressure of higher stakes—she was confident in her hand.

"Seven thousand," said Bryan.

"Ten thousand," I replied.

Another call from Alicia.

Bryan deliberated. Finally, he said, "twelve thousand, five hundred."

"I'll call that," I said. Alicia sighed in relief.

Bryan laid down his cards. Nine of diamonds and four of diamonds. He'd almost had the straight flush. But *almost* doesn't win hands.

"Flush," he declared, a note of satisfaction in his voice.

Alicia dropped her cards as well, but mournfully. She had the straight.

All eyes were on me—just how I like it. Slowly, I lowered my hand. "Full house," I said, as sweetly as I could.

Bryan's eye twitched. I winked and began scooping up my winnings.

And the game continued.

Our system wasn't foolproof—Camilla took a hand soon after when I'd thought she was bluffing—but through some combination of my tapping and Addie's setups my pile of chips grew slowly, hour by hour, both in size and height, forming different-colored stacks and drawing the ire and envy of the other players, Bryan especially. Every hand I won, he took as a personal affront to his skill. We often found ourselves the last two people in a round, raising the stakes two or three times over before throwing down. His hands were good, but mine were somehow better, time after time.

It was after a particularly "lucky" round in which I had a higher-value full house than Bryan that George decided enough was enough. "Could I see that deck, please?"

Play stopped. Addie paused mid-shuffle.

"Pardon?" she said, with the perfect mix of disbelief and condescension.

"Erm, not accusing you of foul play, Roxy," George stammered, wilting beneath Addie's gaze. "Just, a new guy shows up, only in town for the one game, and gets this lucky, over and over? Seems a little suspicious. Maybe he rigged the deck somehow, without you knowing, or . . . well, maybe it's nothing. But I'd like to take a peek, is all."

There was a murmur of general assent from the others, who'd been watching their chips diminish all night. Suddenly, a whole lot of people were looking at Addie expectantly, and if one even got the slightest bit suspicious, and noticed Addie's face wasn't quite the same as Annette's . . .

"Wait!" I said as forcefully as I could, to draw attention away from her. It worked—everyone looked at me instead. "Sorry if I've hit something of a lucky streak tonight, but surely this isn't necessary." I smiled winningly at an array of people doing their best to skewer me with their eyeballs. Behind them, Addie's hand darted under the table for maybe two seconds.

"I'd say it's *very* necessary," said Bryan, suddenly

looking quite dangerous. "I think we all agree." He turned back to Addie, whose hands were safely back above the table. "Pass him the deck, Roxy."

Addie tossed George the deck, her every feature radiating contempt. "The deck is fine, I examined it myself. Two years, I run this game. Never have I taken advantage. I keep the game safe. I keep the players happy. But that means nothing when you start losing money. Desperate for someone to blame besides your own bad luck."

George riffled through the deck, then peered at each card while running his forefinger over their surfaces. Finally, he looked up, utterly abashed. "It's fine."

"Of course it is," said Addie witheringly.

"Let me see," snapped Bryan, and all but grabbed the deck out of George's hands.

"Check his pockets," suggested Jordan from the other side of the table. "He's snowing us. He's gotta be. That rush a few hands back was *impossible* luck."

"Hey now," I said, holding up my hands in a

nothing-to-hide gesture. "I'm not comfortable with that."

Not that my pockets held anything incriminating, but the *principle*'s the thing. I wasn't gonna let these people's hands near me until they sweet-talked me a little.

"You know what *I'm* not comfortable with?" said Felton. "Getting cheated."

"Hear, hear," said Camilla.

Everyone was looking at me again.

"I," I said, swallowing, "am feeling very *not safe* right now. Roxy, you said this was a safe environment."

George put a large hand on my shoulder and gripped me with a force beyond most men his age. "Stand up." The tall man Addie had been talking to earlier—who it turns out *was* security—cleared his throat menacingly. Somehow, he'd gotten next to me without anyone noticing.

The hand on my shoulder withdrew.

"I'm *not* cheating you," I said with all the sincerity I could muster.

"Yeah," sneered Jordan. "Like we're gonna—"

"He's telling the truth," Bryan sighed.

Everyone—myself included—looked at him in shock.

"I know every trick in the book," said Bryan. Every word sounded like it was plunging a dagger into his chest as he spoke it. "And a few it doesn't have. I've been watching this jerkass like a hawk, and he's not messing with his cards. Maybe he slipped one by me, but not enough to win like he's been doing. And the deck's clean too. Looks like it's all luck." He smiled at me, and there was no mercy in it. "But luck can always turn before the night ends."

With that, he handed the deck back to Addie. "Let's keep this game going," he said, and Addie started dealing like nothing had happened, wearing a haughty "I-told-you-so" expression. My heart was pounding at a thousand beats a minute. That'd been *far* too close.

My next hand was promising—a pair of sixes. And when Addie revealed the flop, there was a six hiding there as well.

I considered. The other players were running low on chips. My wealth easily accounted for roughly two-thirds of the table's total assets. Bryan held most of the rest—he'd managed to win a high-stakes hand several rounds back. He was clearly on tilt when it came to me, so I could probably draw him into a bidding war.

This could be the last hand I had to win.

I tapped the table seven times. Addie probably didn't need me telling her what to do, but it wouldn't hurt if she knew I was on board. Besides, I didn't want some stupid miscommunication to ruin this chance.

Bidding closed at $600, with six other people in. The others didn't have the funds to play the odds anymore.

Addie burned a card, then flipped the turn.

I squinted at the jack of clubs, trying to rearrange what I was seeing into a six.

My brain crashed.

I'd signaled for a six. There was no six. There was no—

I forcefully *dragged* my thoughts back in line—rebooted, as it were. I couldn't afford a freak-out right now, I had to figure out what the hell had just happened. *Without* asking Addie, or even looking at her.

Bidding passed to me at $800 and I called without giving the decision the consideration it deserved. I just didn't have the bandwidth.

Eight of clubs. Nine of clubs. Six of diamonds. Jack of clubs.

Something had to make sense here.

No, I was being silly. Of *course* Addie wouldn't deal the other six until the river. She was setting up a situation where it was easy to make a straight or a flush, so she could drop the possibility of a four of a kind *after* people had committed money. Wanting it right away'd been shortsighted.

This set me up for a knockout blow, and I was ready to oblige.

The bidding was at $1,200 when it came back. I raised to $2,000, and watched the bid go around. Claudette raised it to $3,500, and Bryan to $4,000.

Two more players folded (plus Camilla, who'd folded back at $800). Which left four active players—Bryan, Slater, and Claudette, plus myself.

Well, everyone *else* was raising. "Six thousand," I said cheerfully. If they wanted to dig their own graves, I'd happily provide a shovel.

"Ten thousand dollars," said Claudette. No trace of a tell showed through her hawk-like face.

Whatever she had, nothing beat four of a kind. Except a straight flush. And Addie wouldn't have let her have a straight flush.

"Fifteen thousand," I said once I had priority. This time, everyone called.

Addie burned two cards, then revealed the river. Again, I saw the pattern of a definitely-not-a-six face card.

I couldn't help it. I shot a glare at Addie.

I regained my composure at once, of course, but the deed was done. Hopefully it'd gone unnoticed. But in that moment, I'd noticed her expression—an alien expression, more suited to Annette's face than hers. But it'd looked a lot like helplessness. Like an apology.

And then it hit me.

Addie didn't have a marked deck anymore.

She'd switched decks under the table to keep from getting caught, and never had a chance to switch back.

Fucking hell.

Slater opened the bidding again, at $1,000. I was up.

I should've folded. Cut my losses.

But I'd promised my friends a million dollars. And I wasn't entirely out of options—I hadn't bluffed much tonight. Hadn't had to, with the dealer on my side. Maybe I could use that.

"Five thousand," I said, pushing in five yellows, trying not to show any nervousness.

"Six thousand dollars," said Claudette. Again, not even a flicker of emotion.

Bryan looked at me, and I thought I saw a smile behind his passive veneer. "Raise you four thousand. That's ten thousand to you, Jake."

Slater—whose first name was apparently Jake—looked at his cards and sighed. "I'm out."

"Fifteen thousand," I said, trying to figure out whether displaying confidence or uncertainty would be more effective. What level were they modeling me at, anyway?

"Fold," said Claudette at last. Matching my bet would've cost her a significant portion of her chips. In fact, she probably shouldn't have stayed in as long as she had.

Down to Bryan and me.

"Thirty thousand," he said. I eyed his pile. Thirty thousand dollars was dipping into his reserves at this point. He didn't have any yellows left.

"Forty-five thousand," I said with grim satisfaction. I could afford to keep going and he couldn't, and we both knew it. But Bryan was still showing nothing but confidence, which was worrying. If he didn't fold, I'd lose the hand, and he wasn't showing any sign of folding. In fact, he wore a smile even more openly now.

He gazed at me a few more seconds, and then . . . "All in."

Fuck.

I forced my voice neutral. "How much *is* that, exactly?"

It added up to $51,400.

This was the point where folding became a good idea.

But . . .

That wouldn't get me back what I'd already committed. It'd save me about $6,500—which wasn't *small*, by any means—but if Bryan was bluffing, I'd still have three of a kind and win.

Were the odds that he was bluffing worth the risk of losing $6,500?

That depended on what those odds *were*. Bryan had been incredibly aggressive this entire round, which *could* signal a bluff. But it could also mean he had the best possible hand, or knew what I was holding.

The probability of those last two were pretty low. And Bryan's behavior *was* consistent with a bluff . . .

"That's the round, then," I said at last, pushing my chips in. "Let's see 'em."

Bryan smiled triumphantly, revealing a king of spades and a four of clubs. "Flush."

I cast down my cards in disgust. I kept my face as smooth and professional as possible, but I felt like a used Kleenex. One that hadn't even made it to the trash can, just left on the floor for people to step on. All that money lost, thanks to my stupid *pride*.

Silence from the watching players, like they were waiting for something.

Silence from Bryan, who looked much less happy than I'd expected.

If the world is out of sync with your expectations, there's something you aren't taking into account, some piece of data you've missed. Bryan's actions were *certainly* out of sync with my expectations.

And that was when I looked more closely at the river.

It still wasn't a six. But it was the queen of clubs.

The fourth club on the table.

I'd missed the forest for the trees. So desperate to

hit four of a kind, so *narrowed in* on that plan, I'd forgotten to consider what else my hand could do.

"Flush," I said at last.

I looked at his four. Then at my six.

Bryan was looking murderous.

The other players were looking envious.

Addie was looking impassive, but I'm sure she was thinking something like, "What a goddamned stud."

I was bubbling with so many endorphins I was surprised they weren't glowing through my skin and making me look like a hedonistic angel. My hands shook slightly as I raked in my winnings.

I can barely remember the next few rounds, so focused was I on my victory. Nobody else's heart was really in it either, and the game was called for the night shortly after. After deducting the hundred thousand I hadn't had at the start, my total was an *incredibly* satisfying one million, four thousand, seven hundred dollars.

Holding that money felt good. It felt right. But it felt more like a beginning than an end.

If only I'd known.

NINE

AFTER ALL THOSE HOURS IN THAT UNDERGROUND room, it was kinda *weird* seeing Addie without her disguise. Her eyes were contact-free and green again, she'd lost an inch discarding the heels, and the face putty had been indefinitely banished to the bathroom sink. She'd cut her hair to help the wig fit better—it was now just longer than a buzz cut—but it still looked more *Addie* than the wig ever had. Finally, most comfortingly, she was holding herself naturally, letting herself smile again. It was a complete transformation, and I had to keep myself from staring.

Not because I cared what the others thought,

mind—but this *was* a celebration, and it'd be rude to focus exclusively on her, when *all* of us had made this caper possible.

"So, lemme get this straight," laughed Kira. "You won the highest-stakes hand of the night . . . by *accident?*"

I shrugged helplessly, which set Z off too. "I'm so good at poker, I win hands by accident."

"He saw your glare," said Addie. She wasn't laughing—she was far too composed—but a smile danced about her lips. "It was too natural to be fake—well, *I* could've faked it, but not you. He must have thought you were mad I hadn't dealt the card you needed . . . "

"Well, that's what I *did* think," I pointed out. "He was *sure* I was bluffing, milking as much cash out of me as possible—actually reading me perfectly."

"Good thing he didn't have a higher club, or you'd have lost most of that pot."

"But that *pot*, though!" Z practically shouted, prompting a, "Shh!" from Kira. "And the other ones too. The whole shebang. One million fucking dollars. Two-fifty thou each."

I love when people acknowledge how great my plans are.

I stood up from my red armchair. "A toast," I said. "To Addie, who would *totally* win best actress for the role of Roxy in 'real life', if Hollywood was ever gonna hear about this."

Addie bowed theatrically, to light applause.

"To Kira, who heroically subdued and babysat not one, but *two* potential loose ends, bravely sacrificing an entire school day in the process. And, you know, *found* everything."

Kira grinned. "Aww, shucks."

Kira had left Annette's house abruptly the moment I'd reported in safely with the money—which I'd only done once I was home, behind three layers of security (high-stakes poker players can be sore losers). Annette would probably go to the police the moment she realized we were gone, but we'd been careful—she'd have nothing but a vague physical description. Not even a motive . . . unless Annette decided to tell them about her illegal poker game. Somehow, I didn't find that likely.

"Last but not least," I concluded, "to Z, whose afternoon of touring the city with a cabbie and helping Richard become the drug smuggler he never wanted to be will surely become the stuff of legend among his many, many friends."

Z shrugged modestly, but I knew he was flattered.

"Don't sell yourself short, boss," said Kira. "You were cool as a cucumber."

"Cooler," Addie assured her.

"A *refrigerated* cucumber," Kira tried, and we all rolled our eyes at her.

"It was pretty nerve wracking," I admitted. "Can't believe I got home safe. I'm still half expecting the mob to crash in here, shoot us all, and take the cash—"

"The mob?" Z looked skeptical.

"Say one player's secretly a mobster, and he's mad I walked away with all his money and calls up his mob pals, and they track me down . . . "

Z considered this with more solemnity than it

deserved. "Nah," he said at last. "A poker game where the winners end up dead doesn't last long. I got a friend who runs one in upper Manhattan."

"Why didn't we use *that* one?" Kira asked.

Z gave her a superior look. "He's my *friend*. I'm not gonna set him up."

"But I'm not—I mean, Richard isn't—a regular," I protested. "Would anyone there really *care* if he—*I*—got bumped off?"

"Sets a bad example," said Z. He took a large sip of coke, which frankly should've been something alcoholic, but Kira's house, Kira's rules. And Kira didn't want her parents to know she drank.

"You're probably safe," said Addie. "But if you want to fake your death and run away to Copenhagen, I'll support you."

"Yeah!" said Kira. "You could fake your death and run away to Copenhagen!"

"I'll think about it," I joked, making a face. "But there's one more job first."

Kira let out a loud war-whoop and punched Addie in the arm. "Hell. yeah. We gonna rob a train?"

"I've got something *crazy* planned," I admitted with a wicked smile. "You guys want in?"

"Don't keep a guy in suspense," said Z. "Let's hear it."

I lowered my voice. "Okay. Step one is you, Z. You find a friend with a hotel. Step two is also you. You get a friend who's over twenty-one to buy us a whole *shit-ton* of booze. Step three is all of us."

Kira smirked. "Best plan ever."

"Step three," I said triumphantly. "Addie plants the booze in someone's room. Then, Z will tell his friend he overheard that someone in another room is real depressed, thinks she's about to try drinking herself to death. The guy investigates, finds the bottles, gets security to intervene. While security's distracted, Kira's gonna pretend to rob the safe. That's when I'll come in and raise the alarm. You run away before you can get the safe open, and I look like a hero. Z's friend the hotel owner will be so grateful, he'll give us the room free. And *then* Addie steals the booze back, and we get rip-roaring drunk."

The others considered this.

"What was the middle part again?" asked Kira.

"I like that plan," said Addie. "Except, let's skip step three. All except the last bit—that can stay."

"Agreed," said Z. "Sorry, Jason, but hers is better. She's the planner now."

"Oh, alright," I said. "If *she's* the planner, and we're rich enough now to bankroll everything without me siphoning funds from Lucas, what's *my* role?"

Z shrugged. "Not my problem. I'm just the guy who knows a guy."

Addie smiled. "Don't worry, you can be the eye candy."

I tried to decide whether that was flattering or offensive, but the implication that Addie found me attractive was reducing my cognitive functions and I was having trouble thinking anything at all.

Luckily, I had Kira to save me. "He makes a pretty good footstool too," she commented, then shoved her feet onto me. "See?"

I pretended to gag, and shook them off. "Jeez, Kira, did you soak your feet in turpentine?"

"Just for you," said Kira, smirking.

"Oh, *come on,*" said Z. "I've been trying to get you to soak your feet in turpentine for *me* for ages. *This* guy comes along, makes you a quarter million dollars, and now *sure*, you'll do it for *him*—"

"Pick a friend and whine to him about it," said Kira waspishly. "These feet don't stink themselves up for just anyone."

I ignored them as they continued their mock argument—it was nothing I hadn't heard a million times over. Addie caught my eye and yawned pointedly.

"You're not allowed to complain yet," I said. "I've been putting up with them for years."

She laughed and scooted her chair closer. "Who's complaining? Gives us some one-on-one time."

"What, so I can tell you how brilliant you were again?

"I'll tell you when I'm tired of hearing it," said Addie. "But who distracted them while I switched the decks?"

"Please. You strapped a backup deck to your leg, not me. And the accent, and the indignation at having your establishment questioned, it was *perfect*—"

"And *you* won the night's biggest pot without my help," said Addie. "You can tell me—I was just moral support, right?"

"I'm gonna go downstairs and grab another drink," said Kira to Z, loudly enough for us to hear. "Coming?"

"Moral support, being the entire backbone of the plan . . . one of those two things."

"What? But—oh, yeah. Yeah, I need another coke," said Z, getting up to follow her. And just like that, I was alone with Addie Bristol.

The mood was *right*, somehow. I was still riding the high of that last big pot, and Addie's body language was more open and relaxed than I'd ever seen it. There were sparks in her eyes, and I wondered if she was feeling it too.

"Really, though," I said. "That whole game, I was thinking what a great team we made. I read your signals, you read mine, and we controlled the fuck outta that table. I'd follow your lead, then step up when you dropped back, and—"

"Yeah," said Addie. "I got that too. Every time you picked up my signals, I wanted to cheer. You wouldn't *believe* how many I swallowed."

I smiled. "I didn't even notice."

"Yes, because you weren't *looking*, except that one time. Everyone else probably thought I had the hiccups."

"Not looking at you was the toughest part," I admitted. Then my brain caught up with my mouth. "I meant—"

Addie raised an eyebrow. There was that goddamned smile again. "*Really?*"

"Like trying to make eye contact, communicating—" But I was floundering, and Addie had no trouble picking up on that. The air was full of tension, a palpable, electric chill that spoke of danger and promise.

"Because the job's over," she said. She stood up gracefully, took a small step closer. "You can look all you want now."

"—Making little signals the other players would've seen—" I was looking anywhere *but* at her, all five-foot-six of her, hands on her hips, raven crew cut, smiling that playful, thin-lipped smile. I was gonna *kill* Kira for leaving me alone with her.

"Or was it the wig?" she asked, walking over to my chair. She crouched by one of the arms. "Do I look better in blond?"

She was so close to me now that not looking would've been awkward, so I forced myself to stare into those piercing eyes. Up close, there were no shadows hooding her gaze, no hidden darkness for her to hide behind. It was blinding, to see her this way. Like stepping out of a cave into the daylight.

"No," I said, my voice steady. "No, you're gorgeous, wig or no wig. Stunning, even."

"I'm glad you think so," said Addie, and she leaned in, brushing her lips against mine.

Everything stopped for a single, glorious second. Including my heart.

It took another few seconds for me to realize her face wasn't in front of mine anymore. She'd continued the leaning motion upwards until she was standing.

I sat there, stunned, barely able to think or even breathe. My lips tingled slightly where hers had passed over them.

"I'm going to see what's keeping Kira and Z," Addie said conversationally, as if nothing had happened. She started towards the door. "I could use another Fanta, anyway."

I worked my throat a few times until it was functioning again. "Ah. Get me one too."

"Sure thing," she responded without looking back. The door opened and closed, and then I was alone in my armchair.

What the *hell* had that been about?

TEN

FOLLOWING THE GAME, SCHOOL WAS A SURREAL experience. I kept feeling this cosmic expectation, like the universe should magically know what I'd done. Whispers in the halls, nods of respect, et cetera. But naturally, nobody knew anything. To my peers, I was still plain old Jason Jorgensen. Life went on.

The exception, of course, being CPC meetings.

"Any ideas about the money?" Kira asked as we took the last few steps to Room 206 together.

"Spending it, or storing it?"

"The second one. Any cool, exciting schemes?"

"Not really. Just deposit in small chunks, and use cash for everything."

Kira let out a long, tortured sigh. "But that's so *boring.*"

"Just another average teenage hardship," I said solemnly, and then knocked three times.

"Who's there?" That was Addie's voice. She'd picked up on our sign-countersign system like she'd been door-keeping for years. "How many baths have you taken today?"

"Jason here. Five baths so far. I'm *impeccably* clean."

"I'm here too," said Kira. "It's Kira. I've only taken four baths, but mine were longer. I'm so clean . . . I'm so clean . . . "

I waited.

" . . . Mr. Clean was like, '*Damn*, girl! You're too clean!'" Kira finished, looking ashamed of herself.

"Alright," said Addie's voice. "Come in. But Kira, that was *awful.*"

"I know," Kira grumbled. "Sorry, okay?"

The door opened, revealing the half-lit

classroom . . . and Addie. I shifted awkwardly—we hadn't discussed last night's capital "I" *Incident,* and I didn't know how to even broach the subject—but she didn't seem uncomfortable in the slightest.

"You're late," she said. She'd already put professor Gildfin in the center of the table. "But I'll ignore it this time. Next time, you're losing gold stars."

"We're not *that* late," Kira groused. "Z isn't even here yet. And his class lets out closest."

"Z and his bathroom breaks," I said. "Probably trying out a new shampoo in the sink."

Kira rolled her eyes. "Course he is. So when he gets here, he'll try and avoid our judgmental gazes. Jason, you gotta say, 'Smooth,' to set me up to say, 'Silky smooth.' Otherwise, it won't make sense. Okay?"

I frowned. "That's the dumbest thing I've heard all day."

"Whatever," said Kira. "Addie, you got my back?"

"Only because I like you," smiled Addie. "So, I heard Jordan—"

Kira and I simultaneously made loud shushing

noises. I gesticulated wildly with my arms while Kira got up and started running mad laps around the table, still shushing as she went.

Addie didn't even blink. She was used to club protocol by now.

"No official business until the full club's assembled," I explained once we'd sat down again.

"Then let's assemble it," said Addie, pulling out her phone and dialing Z.

Long seconds passed. "Went to voicemail," she said at last, and started typing up a text instead.

A minute ticked by in silence, and still no reply came. Addie's mouth had set in a firm line. "Have either of you *seen* Z today?"

"Calm down," said Kira. "He's kinda late. Nothing to worry about."

"No," said Addie. "I'm . . . never mind, I can't describe it."

I frowned. "Do you know something we don't?"

"I don't know anything," said Addie hesitantly. "It's just a feeling. In my stomach, like I've swallowed too much cold water. Something feels wrong."

Kira and I looked at each other. "Are you sick?" I asked, confused.

Addie shook her head. "I get like this sometimes. It would come in handy when I stole things . . . strange hunches before things went awry. It doesn't always happen, but it's never wrong. Ever. I know it sounds stupid—"

It did. But Addie had opened my mind to the possibility that something *was* wrong, and now I couldn't dismiss it.

I dialed a guy I'd had a group project with once. He picked up right away. "Hello?"

"Hey, Jackson, Jason here. You have English with . . . " I racked my brain for the right name, " . . . Zale, right?"

"Yeah, why?"

"You seen him today?"

"Lemme think . . . Nope."

"Right. Thanks. Bye."

"Bye." *Click.*

I looked right at Addie. "For now, trust your

instincts." My brain was chilling over, giving my thoughts icy clarity. "Something *is* wrong."

Z was missing.

The obvious hypothesis was that he was sick or otherwise occupied—but he would've told us, were that the case. And if was anything *too* serious, the school would've been notified and word would've spread—we'd have heard the news *hours* ago.

Maybe someone from the game was out for revenge. Except Z hadn't *been* at the game. They'd have come after *me*, or maybe Addie. There was a slim possibility that someone'd found me, discovered my relationship to Z, and kidnapped him to get at me, but that added all sorts of complexity penalties.

So find the point in the plan where Z was involved and think *who*—

Well, that made it obvious, didn't it? But that didn't make any *sense*. The guy was a *tech CEO*, for Christ's sake, ranking somewhere below Chihuahuas on the threat scale.

"Kira," I said calmly. "When you were infiltrating

the poker game's website, you also checked out Richard's inbox, right?"

"Yup," said Kira. "To get his flight info. Wasn't that hard. He chose a really dumb password."

"Check it again. Please."

Kira popped her laptop open. Soon, I was looking at Richard's inbox. Kira scrolled down a bit, and I scanned the subject headings, but nothing stood out—besides the sheer volume of Viagra ads.

"Outbox," I said, and Kira obliged. There was very little from the past few days, and definitely nothing relating to Z's disappearance.

"He's got a draft saved," said Kira, and clicked the drafts folder.

Sure enough, there was one message, with the subject heading "Hello".

With shaking fingers, I indicated it. Kira clicked.

The three of us read in silence.

Hello, my friends,

What a pity I couldn't make the poker

game! From what I heard, it sounded like a lot of fun. Apparently, I had the most fun of anyone, but I don't remember it that way. I was finalizing my release from prison at the time, you see.

It was a clever little stunt you pulled. You must have had to do all sorts of things, like access my e-mail. Since I have no other way to contact you, I'll have to hope you read this at some point. It would be so sad for your friend if you didn't.

That reminds me. It occurred to me, while I was waiting for my release to be processed, that the only person who got close enough to my bag to plant the cocaine was the taxi driver's assistant. Giving him such a conspicuous role was a mistake, I think you'll agree. Long story short, he's spending some quality time with me now. He's not the most gracious guest, though, and I'd rather have the money you won under my name. So that's the deal.

Give me $1,100,000, and you can have your assistant taxi driver.

I realize I'm not leaving you this message where you're likely to find it, but I trust you're smart enough to check here eventually. I'm generous, so I'll give you 72 hours from the time this draft was made to contact me. After that, I can't guarantee your associate's safety. I await your e-mail with the strongest anticipation.

Love and kisses,

R. Trieze

"Well, shit," said Kira at last. "Fuck that fucking bullshit."

"Seconded," I said dryly.

Kira's not the most eloquent, but in this situation, her sentiment was more than appropriate. This was no tech CEO's letter—more straight-up movie villain.

I'd underestimated Richard Trieze.

"When did he write this?" asked Addie, peering at the screen.

I pointed. "About four hours ago. We got lucky."

"That gives us three days."

Kira looked at Addie like she'd suggested we dance down the hallway naked singing Christmas carols. "I think you mean, 'That gives us plenty of time to whisper tearful goodbyes to our armfuls of cash and leave it in a pile on Richard's doorstep.'"

"I'll leave *something* in a pile on his doorstep," snapped Addie. "Seriously? We're going to pay up? We're better than that."

"Ripping off gamblers is one thing," I said. "A full rescue mission is another."

Addie glared daggers at me. "All that work, for nothing? Is this the future you envisioned for the club, Jason?"

"I can try to figure something out," I said, "but I can't even think how we'd *find* Z. And *then* if we were caught, they'd learn who we were, and we'd never be safe again. Taking the deal's probably safest."

Saying that hurt. I was giving my biggest success

up as a lost cause, and that was a full-body blow to my pride. But what other choice did we have?

"Sounds like fun. Can I change my vote?"

"Kira."

"Kidding, boss. Kidding."

Addie shook her head. "You don't get it. Neither of you get it." There was an edge to her voice that hadn't been there before.

"It was a long shot anyway," I said tiredly. "I even half expected something like this to happen before we were through. We back off *now*, we don't really lose anything, as long as we're careful and don't let Richard get too close. Money's nice, but . . . "

I trailed off, losing my train of thought. Addie was *shaking*.

"If you won't help, I'll do it myself," she said tightly. She pressed her lips together so hard they turned pale, and took a deep breath, trying to calm herself.

And then the breaths came faster, more frequently, and the shaking was coming from deeper within her, and something had *broken* in her face, like all the emotions she held so tightly every minute of her existence had escaped their prison at once.

Finally, words came, but they were jerky and disconnected, like Addie was trying to hold them back.

"Don't understand—my *mamá*—gambles. Too much. It—she loses, can't stop—always in debt. I was—helping, but—big, this time. Too much. Can't pay. Not . . . not without—"

She stopped as abruptly as she'd started, face flooded with shame and self-directed fury. The room was frozen in shock.

Kira broke the stalemate. She stood up from her computer and wrapped one arm around Addie's unresponsive shoulders. "Hey. Don't worry about it."

She gave me a look that said, "Shut up and let me handle this." Normally I'd object, but in this situation . . .

"We're gonna go save Z, alright?" she said. "You're one of us now. We're gonna help you out."

ELEVEN

LUNCHTIME HAD ENDED A HALF-HOUR AGO, BUT WE had no intention of returning to our classes.

We'd switched rooms in case the teachers sent someone, but more likely, they'd mark our absence and report it to the main desk, where the notification would be "lost in the bureaucratic shuffle" and never revisited.

Again, we've been doing this for years.

Addie was still flushed, but she was much calmer now that Operation Save Z was underway. I could hardly say no after that display. I got the sense she'd kept that secret bottled up all her life for fear of other people taking advantage of it, and that making it public had been incredibly harrowing. We basically had two options—help her, or shit all over her hopes and dreams.

Kira and I hadn't pressed her for more details, even though I had questions upon questions for her. We weren't waiving the traditional favor owed, though. And we could probably convince Z that *he* owed us favors too—provided we managed to rescue him.

So I'd sat, considering the situation, for five minutes. Proposing solutions would come later. Simply understanding the problem was its own task. Five minutes later, I'd decided the problem looked something like *this*.

Complication One: Z's whereabouts were unknown.

Complication Two: Richard's defenses, if any, were unknown.

Complication Three: The defenses themselves, if any.

Complication Four: Keeping our identities secure throughout.

Kira was currently working on the first. Her

fingers moved across her keyboard in a blur, and death metal kept escaping through her heavy-duty headphones. Every so often, she'd break the silence with an impressive string of profanities. Addie and I sat next to her, lost in our own little worlds.

I was playing back every interaction I'd had with Richard, every piece of information we'd dredged up. Anything at all that could be useful. As you might remember, there wasn't much to work with.

"What's the plan once we find him?" Addie asked suddenly.

I frowned. "Depends where he is. But some things make sense no matter what. For instance, the probability of you doing recon is around point-nine."

"Recon, I can do."

"After that, assuming Z's being held in a conventional fashion, you either go in again to free him or go in with Kira so she can beat up anyone who'd prefer you *didn't*."

"Motherfucking shitweasel son of a cocksucking titbitch!" That was Kira, of course, still oblivious to meatspace. I raised my eyebrows and Addie started giggling. She sobered almost immediately.

"I've been thinking about everything Brad said while I was at Annette's, but none of it's useful."

Something tugged at my memory. "Wait."

I hadn't thought my conversation with Brad important, as Richard hadn't been involved . . . but then, he *had* been involved, in a way. From my end.

"They had a safe house," I said breathlessly, remembering the conversation all at once. "Brad told me. It was . . . one-eighty-something . . . one hundred eighty-four Eleventh Avenue. In Chelsea. Maybe that's where—"

And then the problem with *that* optimistic thought presented itself, crushing my hope mid-blossom. "But Richard will've talked to Brad."

"Brad was smart," Addie said wearily. "If he gave you the address, he'll remember it isn't safe anymore."

"Let's reconstruct the sequence of events," I said. "Richard's released and calls Brad. Brad's pissed— far as he's concerned, Richard betrayed him. Richard talks him down, explains what happened to him. Brad finds out from his poker buddies what happened there, and tells Richard. Richard figures out Z framed him, finds Z somehow, and grabs him. Wants to take him to the Chelsea safe house. Brad says no, it's been compromised . . . "

"Which results in an evacuation," Addie cut in. "Any moment, we could give that address to the authorities. By now, it's been stripped of any clues we could've found."

The two of us sat defeated for several seconds. "We don't know that," I volunteered.

"No. We don't," admitted Addie. "We could check it out after school. But I'd bet my take that one hundred eighty-four Eleventh Avenue will be as empty as this classroom's *supposed* to be."

I knew she was right. "No bet."

"This shit's ridiculous," said Kira suddenly, ripping off her headphones.

"Report," I said.

"Did everything I could think of," Kira growled. "Richard's using a new account. Poked around, found it, couldn't get in, or trace the access point, or do the next hundred fucking things I tried. He got *careful.*"

"Our opponents are prepared this time," I pointed out. "That makes them dangerous."

"Don't I know it," Kira snarled. "Haven't hit this many dead ends since the pumpkin farm. I'm piss out of ideas. How 'bout you, boss?"

I shook my head. "Nothing worth mentioning. Though we have three days wiggle room—we can afford to sleep on it for a night. If nobody has a real solution by then, we'll start worrying for real."

"Boss, I tried *everything.* There's nothing left to think of. Even accessed New York's traffic cams to try and spot the kidnapping, before I remembered how much footage I'd have to wade through. I even e-mailed Imperial Tech to see—"

"You have traffic cam footage?"

"That, and all sorts of other cameras too. These monkeys connected their CCTVs to the Internet and hid them behind a simple *password.*" Kira's voice was dripping with contempt. "But it's useless.

They could've grabbed him anywhere in the city. There's *thousands* of cameras and they don't even cover every—"

"Let's say I knew where to look."

For the first time, Kira looked away from the screen and at me. Addie mirrored her, the same silent question on both faces.

"Hypothetically, sorry," I amended hastily. "I don't *actually* know. Could you track the car to where they'd taken him?"

"Sure, that was the whole point," said Kira. "You just follow it from cam to cam . . . boss? You're smiling."

"Again, hypothetically speaking," I said, aiming this question more at Addie, "if Richard and his team had to abandon a location in a hurry, and I knew the address, would the odds that they'd go wherever they're holding Z be large enough to justify looking through that cam footage?"

Kira's brow wrinkled. "Run that by me again."

"Jason, that's *brilliant!*" Addie gasped.

"It is, and I am. Kira, get me satellite of one

eighty-four Eleventh Avenue and the surrounding area, then tell me the make, model, and color of any car parked there."

"One eighty-four Eleventh Avenue," repeated Kira, jamming her headphones back over her ears and fiddling with the computer volume. "And you got this address . . . how?"

"From Brad," I said. "I'll explain later. Lemme know if you find the car, then check the cams for it. I want its final destination, because I'm pretty sure Z'll be there."

"I see a car," Kira reported. "Blue SUV."

"Re-access the security files for that area and play them back."

There were several more moments of tense silence as Kira worked, moments that stretched slowly into minutes as Addie and I watched hopefully. Kira was swearing much less now . . .

"Got it!" she yelled. "It left about eight hours ago, heading west. You can follow it on the cams after that, until . . . "

She pulled up a screengrab. There was the car, mid-turn.

"After that, there's nothing—no more cams. But the area's small enough that we can grid search for the car, no problem."

She slapped the table with both palms. "And *that's* how you fucking do it!"

"Kira with the *skills*!" said Addie, punching Kira's shoulder. "What's next?"

"I *was* thinking we'd check it out after school," I said with a devil-may-care smirk. "But why wait?"

TWELVE

THE CAR PULSED WITH AN ELECTRONIC BEAT THAT threatened to wrench the entire machine apart. My ears were ringing—possibly a defense mechanism against the utter lack of musicality they were being subjected to—and my hands, jammed tight over my ears, were feeble help in the face of the tasteless onslaught that poured ceaselessly from the speakers.

Addie's lips were clamped in a thin line of stoic disapproval, but her eyes betrayed her pain. Every so often, we exchanged glances and silently reaffirmed our mutual suffering. We didn't make the rules of teenage etiquette, but we *do* abide by them, and a non-negotiable driver's privilege is picking the music.

You'd think this rule had its limits. It doesn't.

You'd think there'd be an exception if only one person in the group can drive, and therefore drives out of necessity rather than courtesy. There isn't.

You'd think if the group leader states in clear terms that the music's making it impossible to determine what course of action will result in the entire group *not* getting shot, he'd receive a more understanding response than, "Suck it up, you big baby," and a toothy grin. He hadn't.

The architect of that insensitive response was bouncing up and down in her seat and punching randomly at the air, in blatant defiance of everything she'd learned in driving school (at least, I hoped she'd been to driving school).

"Alright!" she shouted over the music rather than, you know, turning it down. "Here's where I lost track of the SUV, so keep your eyes peeled!"

With that, she spun the steering wheel with one hand and pumped the brakes, slowing the car to a much more manageable speed. To my surprise, we didn't speed up again—Kira let the car coast slowly, so Addie and I could see each car as we passed.

Kira had heavily annotated a printout map detailing the likely area the SUV was in, based on traffic patterns, alternate routes, and camera placement. The area wasn't large, but if it didn't contain the car, we'd have to expand our search . . . or check the garages on foot. Both would take precious time.

We passed car after car and building after building. My eyes were just starting to hurt from the strain of constantly looking, when—

"There!" said Addie excitedly. "That's it!"

I whipped my head around and saw it, parked on the road in front of a large house. It was definitely *a* blue SUV. But then, what were the odds that there were two identical cars so close to each other? "Nice one," I said.

Kira parked. The car stopped. The musical torture ended.

Addie and I exhaled identical, relief-filled sighs, then grinned at each other.

"Last stop," said Kira. "Everybody out."

I opened the door and stepped out of the car. Half a block down and across the street, the SUV stood parked. Addie walked over to me, letting her gaze pass naturally over the house as she did.

"We sure that's it?" she asked.

"Nope," I said. "Go find out."

Kira and I end up alone together on the sidelines more often than not. Z prefers to approach his friends alone, and company actively *hampers* Addie's sneaking, so leaving us behind is logical. Yet . . . while Kira's great, I kinda wish it was Addie, you know?

Yeah, I admit it. I was still thinking about the whole almost-kiss thing—even though Z's predicament was the clear priority.

If Addie was thinking the same, she didn't show it—but then, she wouldn't. "No problem," she said. "It'll be fun."

"Okay. Keep your phone on silent—we'll be in touch." I turned to Kira. "We're on standby. If Addie wants us in, we go in."

Kira cracked her knuckles slowly and deliberately, one at a time. "Action?"

"Action. Addie, if you're worried for any reason, don't hesitate to disengage, alright?"

No answer. I turned back around, knowing what I'd see. Sure enough, Addie was already gone. "Unbelievable. Who does she think she is, *Batman?*"

Kira got real serious. "Holy shit, what if she is?"

Believe it or not, she spent the next few minutes trying to convince me that Addie was, in fact, Batman. Her main argument was, "There's no evidence she isn't," despite my spending most of the conversation providing it. Finally I reached for my phone to ask Addie to tell Kira she wasn't Batman only to see a missed text from her. I'd forgotten I'd turned my phone to silent preemptively.

2 guards with guns. somethings going on.

I read it three times, but it kept saying the same thing.

Guards.

Guns.

I'd expected a dog and an ADT system at most. I guess Z's being literally kidnapped should've clued me in—we were apparently dealing with the most dangerous tech CEO in the *world*. I almost wondered if we'd gotten the wrong house, stumbled on some unrelated conspiracy by accident.

Addie's next message a few minutes later didn't help matters.

no z so far.

But then, Z wouldn't necessarily be here even if this *was* the right place. Richard could have multiple safe houses, for example. Or the Chelsea safe house could be used by many different people and we'd followed the wrong car.

The light on my phone blinked twice. Another message.

i see richard

That eliminated that last possibility. Three more messages followed in quick succession.

hes mad we havent respond yet

and he cant get more info from z

sounds like zs here

I sent a message back. Find him.

"He's in there," I said to Kira, and she smiled. It wasn't a normal expression for Kira—well, *smiling* was, but this smile was different. It was warm and caring.

"He's a good kid," she said. "Just don't ever tell him I said that, you hear?"

"My lips are sealed, as long as Addie never hears a word about—"

"Boss. *Boss.* You know I'm behaving myself."

"Fine," I sighed. "You're a paragon of subtlety."

"That's me," said Kira. "So, how's things? With Addie, I mean."

She gave me a piercing look, like she already knew the answer.

"I . . . haven't had time to think about it recently."

She *definitely* didn't believe me. Which was perfectly fair. This is *me* we're talking about—I *always* have time to think.

Also, there's the part where I actually *was* lying.

"Better go for it," she warned. "Keep stalling and you'll miss your chance."

"Alright. As soon as we get Z, I'll talk to her."

About what the hell happened when we sort-of kissed, I finished in my head.

Another message.

count 4 guards so far.

Still wondering what deity I'd made jealous enough to call for armed guards, I relayed the information to Kira.

"Big deal. Send me in, I'll kick their asses."

"They have guns," I said patiently.

Kira snorted. "So?"

"So you could walk into that house with nothing but your bare hands and take down four armed men? That's what you're saying?"

"Only one way to find out," said Kira, shrugging casually.

She said it with such blasé confidence that I almost gave her the go-ahead before I came to my senses.

"The situation doesn't call for muscle," I said patiently. "Surprise is on our side, but the moment we use it, our advantage is gone. They have no reason to be on alert, so we won't give them one."

"I'm like a fucking DD," Kira grumbled. "Except nobody ever gets drunk."

"Alright, alright. I'll make sure every plan from now on includes minimal driving and a whole lot of gratuitous violence."

Kira beamed. "Thanks, boss."

I was weighing the pros and cons of pointing out that I'd been kidding when my phone's light flashed again.

z in basement. 2 more guards. z hurt.

I felt a strange combination of relief and dread. Z was here and alive. That meant we could save him. On the other hand, there were a bunch of people between us. And they had guns.

"She found Z," I said.

Kira punched the air like it owed her money. "Yes!"

"He's hurt," I continued. "Two guards by him. Can you take two guards?"

"Can Appargus take three dicks in his ass at once?"

"How—no, *why*—never mind."

To Addie, I typed, Hold position if you can. Guide us in?

mybe. guards not esp alert.

I considered this. "Alright, Kira," I said at last. "You're getting your wish. We're going in."

Her face split into a wide grin.

I turned towards the car to make a few final preparations. "Do whatever you need. I'll be ready in ten."

Going in without contingencies would've been stupid, after all. It was nice knowing that just in case things went belly-up, I'd have options. And setting them up didn't exactly *cost* me anything . . . well, nothing but the ten minutes, anyway.

Ready, I texted Addie when I was done.

Her response was immediate. ill let u kno. b rdy any sec.

We waited maybe fifteen minutes longer in silence. At least, *I* did—Kira spent most of it alternating between making sound effects with her mouth and growling song lyrics. Needless to say, Addie's next text was a relief.

now. west guard on break. side door unguarded/ unlocked. do not aprch front.

"Follow me," I said, and walked purposefully into the neighboring yard, approaching the target house from the side.

Addie was right about the side door being unlocked. It slid open to reveal a small antechamber, which contained a refrigerator and just enough space for two people to stand comfortably.

In fridge room, I sent.

The response came quickly. do not stop, guard rm

"Keep moving," I muttered.

break over in 4 mins

The antechamber led to a longer hallway with several doors. I looked at them helplessly and reached for my phone, hoping Addie could guide us—

She'd anticipated my need.

open 2nd door 2 yr rght

I did so, revealing a room with a washing machine and a dryer. I motioned Kira in and shut the door after her.

Immediately, everything went black around us.

Resisting the urge to verbally flagellate myself, I groped blindly for several confused seconds until I found the switch.

There. Now it was just me, Kira, and two clothes-washing appliances cuddling up against each other in the cramped quarters. Safe, for the moment.

We made it. Tell us how to get to the basement.

I waited for several seconds, and then the replies started pouring in.

guard back soon. let him pass

will guard fridge rm, look out door wndw. no need 2 engage, just be quiet

open last door on left. u r now in main house, study

rich. +others in lvng rm. do nt distrb.

cross study &open door 2 bedrm on yr left

wait there

I internalized these instructions, then responded. Got it.

We waited quietly until we heard footfalls closer

and closer, then farther again down the hall, then a door opening and closing. I waited several more tense seconds, then motioned Kira to open the door.

We tiptoed down the hall. The linoleum did little to mask our footsteps, but no doors opened suddenly, and no raised voices demanded we stop, so we must've been moving quietly *enough*. After what felt like forever, we reached the bright green door at the far end and slowly eased it open.

The next room's theme was wood. Wooden floorboards, two wooden steps up to the room's level, and beautiful wood furniture—two ornately carved desks, one sporting a laptop, and a single small chair. Three stained-wood bookshelves held hundreds of faded books, neglected by their owner.

"I think this is the study," Kira couldn't resist muttering.

We crossed the room to the unpainted wooden door and I opened it a crack, peering through to make sure I had the right door. The room contained a bed, a dresser, and approximately zero angry guards—perfect.

"What now?" muttered Kira, following me into the small bedroom.

"Lemme check."

"No need," said a calm voice from beyond the door. My heart stopped for a second before I realized it was Addie. Kira, realizing the same thing, slowly relaxed out of the combat stance she'd immediately assumed.

"Thought I'd meet you here instead," Addie explained, poking her face into view.

"Jesus fucking Christ," said Kira. "I almost punched your face off."

I took a deep, calming breath—and then another when the first wasn't enough. "I'm really, really glad it's you. Fill us in."

"Z's in the basement. There are stairs off the main hallway towards the front, just past the living room."

"Guards?"

"One per doorway—front, back, and side," said Addie. "Two guarding Z, and one currently with Richard in the living room . . . last I checked, anyway."

"And do we know why Richard has goons with guns hanging around here? Or who owns the house?"

"Nothing so far. You're right, it's weird. Sounds like they're all scared of him, though. This guy's bad news. Which you'd think *someone* would've picked up when scouting him . . . "

I winced. "Point taken. How do we get to Z?"

"Sneak past the living room, down the stairs, loose Kira on the guards—" Kira smiled widely, "—and we'll go from there. Then we just need a way out."

"I'll think of something," I said reassuringly.

"Toughest part'll be the living room," said Addie. "Leave that to me. And remember, if we get caught, we're dead."

On that inspiring note, we walked back into the study. Addie catwalked to the door and pressed her ear against it. Looking satisfied, she opened the door a crack and peered through. Finally, she opened it the rest of the way and beckoned us. We followed, moving as noiselessly as we could.

We found ourselves in a long hallway with a high ceiling, bookended by the front door and one that led further into the house. From the direction of the front door, I heard voices.

We crept down the hallway until we reached the living room. The voices were louder now, and if any of us were brave enough to put their head around the corner, we'd no doubt see their owners. More to the point, *they*'d see *us*.

Addie held up her hand. *Wait.* She started back the way we'd came. When she reached the door at the end of the hallway, she looked back to make sure we weren't following, winked, and vanished into the bowels of the house.

Kira and I waited as per instructions, painfully aware of how exposed we were. If the front guard decided to say hi to his buddies in the living room . . .

But we didn't have to wait long before the sound of shattering glass echoed from further inside. I heard, "The hell—" from the living room, and bodies shifting, moving away from us. Kira and I looked at each other, then started down the hallway.

As I passed the open entrance, I couldn't resist a peek inside. A large and imposing man was opening a door at the other end of the room while Richard looked on. "See anything?" Richard asked.

"No," the man responded. "Broken vase. Dunno what happened. Wind, maybe."

Safety lay behind the lip of the entrance, and I didn't even breathe until Kira and I made it past.

We stood there for a few minutes, trying to decide if we should wait for Addie, or—in Kira's case—struggling to stay quiet and not make fun of me. Thankfully, Addie saved us the trouble of deciding by finally reappearing.

She approached the entrance to the living room, then dropped to the ground and peeked in. Apparently happy with what she saw, she crawled across to the other side, never making more noise than a falling hair.

A few more steps put us in front of a door. Slowly, cautiously, Addie reached out a hand and eased it open, revealing a dark staircase. Addie motioned us in, then followed and shut the door behind us, leaving us in darkness. Which was just as quickly replaced by dim, flickering light as Addie hit the light-switch.

"Alright," said Addie in a low voice. "At the bottom is a small storage room with three doors. They're holding Z in the left room. Ready?"

We were.

The basement was a jumble of holiday decorations and camping equipment, with low doors leading in the other three cardinal directions. Addie pointed towards the left one—redundantly, I suppose, but reminders are never *bad*.

We rooted through the debris for anything that might do some damage. I found a long candlestick, Addie discovered a Swiss army knife among the camping gear, and Kira ended up with a detached wooden chair leg. Thus armed, we positioned ourselves by the door.

Addie held up her free hand with her middle three fingers up. Then two fingers. Then one finger.

She opened the door, and Kira surged forward, chair-leg set to swing—but she stopped so suddenly I bumped into her. I peeked around her and saw two guns pointed at her chest. Needless to say, I stopped as well.

On the bright side, Z was definitely here too—I could see him. His eyes were wide, and his lips were working madly around a strip of cloth. I gave him a reassuring nod.

Behind him was a small black-and-white TV, happily displaying the very basement we'd just come through. They'd seen us coming.

"Take a seat," one of the men said gruffly, gesturing with his gun next to Z.

For a moment, I thought we could still salvage this. Then I heard loud footsteps coming from the basement staircase, and knew it was hopeless. I took the offered seat.

"This rescue was a lot cooler in my head," I admitted.

"Don't sweat it, boss," said Kira. "There's only two. Moment I see an opening, I'll save all our asses. Again."

Addie backed into the room slowly, followed by four more guards. Scowling, she sat down next to us.

"Six," Kira amended. "There're only six."

"Just banter for now," I muttered. "See how much they'll take. I'll think of something."

Kira reached tentatively for Z's gag. When none of the gunmen shot her for moving, she untied it.

"Nice to see y'all," said Z. His voice was hoarse and dry.

"Jesus, dude," said Kira. "This is like, the worst I've *ever* seen your hair. What have they done to you?"

"They actually offered me some stuff when I asked, but I turned it down. It was all off-brand crap. I was better off with nothing."

"Z, in?" I asked. For the first time ever, he shook his head.

On an intellectual level, I'd known it'd happen eventually. But it still felt like the universe had gone *wrong* somehow. And why'd it have to be at the worst possible moment?

"You got us," I said to the gunmen. "Congratulations. Now what?"

"I'm glad you asked," said Richard himself, with an entrance timed so perfectly he must've been waiting outside the door, listening for a good time to enter. And boy, did he look pleased with himself.

He was quite comfortable among his minions, gesturing for them to tie us to our seats with an ease born of familiarity. And yet he seemed out of place, scrawny and unthreatening beside his *highly* intimidating groupies. They didn't break expression once as they tied us, but Richard's face sported a madcap smile. He looked like a clown in a haunted house—clashing horribly with the aesthetic, but at home nonetheless.

"Well, well, well," said Richard slowly, looking at us all in turn. He focused his gaze on me. "It's an honor to meet you, Mr. Trieze—but wait, I'm sorry. *I'm* Mr. Trieze. So despite what you claimed at that poker game, I'd say you're lying. And I *hate* liars."

His eyes swept Addie up and down. "And here, we have the lovely Roxy herself. It's a pleasure to meet face to face. I'm sure the real Roxy would agree—she's *dying* to meet you as well."

"And a plus-one," he said, looking at Kira dismissively. "But—no, *you're* the one who stole my cab so rudely when I first arrived in this lovely city." He smiled tightly. "I wasn't expecting you to indulge my hospitality—color me pleasantly surprised. I would've settled for being mailed or wired the money, but you were kind enough to bring it yourselves . . . with, no doubt, an apology."

Silence.

"You *do* have the money, right?"

Another awkward silence. Richard's smirk widened.

"Well then."

"Goddammit, Blondie," I said. "I thought *you* had it."

"I told Sue to grab it before we left," said Kira. "Sue, you saying you didn't?"

Addie shrugged. "Must've slipped my mind."

I looked helplessly at Richard. "Sorry 'bout that. Our mistake. Now, maybe you can let us go, and we can get the money from where it's hidden and bring it back here?"

Richard's eyebrows raised. "So you *do* have the money hidden somewhere."

"Did I say that?" I countered.

"Yeah," said Addie. "You did."

"Well, I didn't mean it."

A high-pitched giggle escaped from between Richard's lips. "I never would've guessed you were just kids! Well, you're playing with grown-ups now. Tell me where you hid my money. You won it in my name, so it really *is* mine, after all."

As you might remember, I was just minutes from acquiescing. But hey, I already told you how this conversation went. You *do* remember, right? If you really need to, you should re-acquaint yourself with that part of the story, because I'm about to keep going like all that just happened. I'll wait. Not like I'm going anywhere.

All done? Alright, then. Let's see how this shakes out.

THIRTEEN

THERE'S ALWAYS A SILVER LINING. TAKE MY PRESENT situation, for example. Sure, I was trapped in Richard's car with the man himself and his laconic, rhinoceros-like assistant, one terse order from painting the upholstery red with my insides, but I couldn't have picked a prettier time of day. The sun was just sinking past the horizon, setting the sky awash with pink-orange hues that I would've appreciated if I hadn't had a gun trained on me. A lot stops mattering at gunpoint.

Or maybe things matter more than ever. I don't know—I'm no philosopher.

Not even my looming mortality, though, was enough to distract me from Richard's gloating.

"You'll *never guess* how easy finding your friend was," he was saying. He'd been going on about how great he was since we left. "The hardest part was tracking down that taxi. You know they all have security cameras in them, just in case? Lucky me, right?"

I'd heard some variation of this story at least six times, but that wasn't gonna stop Richard from telling it again. He'd made me apologize for kidnapping Brad ten times over, and I'm sure he'd do it again next time he was bored.

At least his voice was helping block out my friends' accusing faces. The hurt in their eyes had made my stomach churn. Especially Addie's. I knew how much this money meant to her.

But I was looking forward to her reaction when— okay, *if*—I got the chance to explain things.

"Then I printed out a few screencaps from the video and asked around. I thought *that* part would be tough, but just about everyone recognized him.

It was only a matter of time before one led me right to him."

"Yeah," I said. "Really clever."

"You must've thought you found the perfect target. Some rich, starry-eyed trust-fund baby."

I'd heard several variations of this as well.

"I was getting my hands dirty before you crawled out of your daddy's nutsack. I've gone up against the mob and *won*, pipsqueak." Richard chuckled. "I thought *they* were after me. Imagine that. Boy, was I relieved when I learned my targets weren't even old enough to buy lottery tickets!"

"That's why we put this plan together," I said sadly. "We wanted to win the lottery, but we weren't old enough to buy the little tickets."

Richard looked at me skeptically, like he'd taken me seriously. Then he burst out laughing. "That was pretty good, kid! What's your name, anyway?"

I chewed on the question for a bit. "Mud," I responded finally. "In the respectable parts of town, anyway. Take this exit."

Richard put his turn signal up. "Gonna tell me where we're headed yet?"

"I just told you, Exit three."

"Please, kid," giggled Richard. "Don't make me spell it out. Our final destination."

"Right, I knew that," I said with a smile of my own. "There's some debate on that score, but Christian theology teaches that there are two main sections of the afterlife—"

"Let me put it this way, Mr. Mud," said Richard. He still sounded jovial, but there was suddenly a dangerous glint in his eyes. "Wanna find out which theology got it right *personally*?"

I swallowed. "You wouldn't kill a kid."

"Try me."

"Alright, alright. We're headed for the docks. Happy?"

"The docks." Richard thought about that for a few seconds. "Sorry, but you'll have to be more specific."

I would've liked to have drawn the conversation

out more, but the big man next to me was a very effective deterrent.

"South Street seaport. Pier Eleven," I said. "*Now are you happy?*"

"You hid the money *there?*"

"It's safe," I said. "I know what I'm doing."

"I guess you didn't have such a bad start, for a rugrat," said Richard begrudgingly. "You even got Brad. He's usually smarter than that. He was pretty mad you knocked him on the head—an apology might be in order."

I rolled my eyes. "Tell him 'sorry' for me."

"Thanks, Mud. He'll appreciate it." Richard laughed again and I had a sudden urge to rip my ears off and stuff them down his throat. It was maybe the most annoying laugh I'd ever heard, and it got worse every time.

"The docks, huh?" said Richard thoughtfully. "Alrighty, then. Surprise me."

Oh, if only he knew. "I've picked up a thing or two in my long life," I said casually.

Richard snorted. "Fucking kids."

Before long, he was gloating again. Outside the window, the sun set and the landscape darkened as Richard's words washed over me in waves. Until . . .

"So this is the place? Pier Eleven?"

I straightened up in my seat and examined our surroundings. There was the pier, just as I remembered it, jutting out into the water like a paved finger. Dark and deserted, like I'd hoped. "This is it," I said.

Richard parked the car. "Field trip!" he said. "Thomas, you're on chaperone duty."

"So *you're* Thomas," I said brightly as I climbed out of the car. "I've heard so much about you."

"Hey, it's quiet time now," said Richard. He motioned with his gun, just in case I needed a reminder that he had it, and stared out across the spread of concrete. "Let's go."

He wasn't giving me a choice. We stepped together down some stairs onto the concrete expanse below. The pier was a maze of storage units and machinery, all of which Richard eyed suspiciously. "I can't believe *this* was your hiding place."

"You must admit, it's the last place you'd look," I pointed out. "I'm leading you right to it and you *still* can't believe it's here."

To that, Richard made no reply.

"So, Thomas," I said as we walked. "Do you talk, or . . . ?"

"No talkie," said Richard. Thomas obeyed.

I sighed. "Just trying to be sociable."

Remember what I said about witty banter earlier? It also keeps you calm in situations where you're leaving the details of your plan up to fate. My heart was pumping a little, but hopefully the nervousness was helping sell the act.

Thomas took the lead, eyes peeled for traps. Richard and I followed side by side, with his weapon wedged firmly into my ribs. The pier was silent, save for footsteps on the concrete and the soft lapping of waves.

"There," I said, pointing to a large metal storage unit. "Behind that."

"Do as the toddler says," Richard ordered, and

Thomas peeked around the corner of the storage unit, then vanished behind it.

If you've noticed by now that most of Richard's jokes involved my age, join the club. It was actually starting to get embarrassing. Like, *really*? Get some new material. He wouldn't last five minutes in a comedy club.

The storage unit formed a thin corridor with its neighbor, too narrow for Richard and I to walk side by side. He let me in first, then stuck his gun into the small of my back. I ushered Thomas along until he'd reached the other side.

"What was the point of that?" Richard muttered, sounding suspicious.

"Just retracing my steps," I whispered back. "This place looks different at night."

I sidled out from behind Thomas towards a large, disused crane, which loomed over the pier. "I remember this crane. Looks very familiar."

Richard was clearly losing his patience. "Why the hell didn't you just walk here first, instead of taking us through that passage?"

"Hm?" I pretended not to understand.

"You're stalling," said Richard. His voice was tight and dangerous—he'd dropped all pretense of jocularity. There was a harsh energy to him suddenly, a glimpse of the man beneath the carefree facade. "I don't have time to wander around a pier all night, Mud. Where'd you hide that *fucking* money?"

I closed my eyes. "Your voice is damaging my calm."

"And my gun is going to damage your head if you don't stop bullshitting me."

"Point taken," I said. My heart was pounding even harder now. I wasn't sure if I'd given the plan enough time, but clearly, it was now or never. "Alright. You want direct? I'll give you direct. There's no money here."

The tension that followed almost killed me, in a very literal sense. But somehow, I felt even calmer now. Better, as well—this new, vicious Richard reminded me of Lucas.

I could play the game against him in good conscience.

Richard pressed the gun against the side of my head. "You've got three seconds, or—"

"Please," I said sardonically. "We've been over this. You won't kill me, because I know where the money is. You'll threaten me, I'll call your bluff, and then you'll threaten one of my friends instead, and as you start the countdown, I'll give in and take you where the money really is." There was a small smile on my face now. It was time to take control of the situation—and hopefully not die in the process. "So let's just skip to the end. Call your men, Dick. Tell them to shoot someone. Make me give in."

I sat down and leaned against one of the crane's legs as Richard pulled out his phone. "You've lost one already," he said, looking murderous. "Maybe you can save the other two if you get me the money within ten minutes, no more games."

I just kept smiling, hoping I looked calm.

With sharp, staccato motions, Richard punched in the number.

I couldn't hear the rings, but I could see his face transition from assured, to confused, to worried as the seconds passed. And with every moment, my hope grew.

Finally, he tore the phone away from his ear and typed the number in again. This time, it was a full minute before he angrily slammed it shut.

"Connection troubles, perhaps," I remarked. "Those newer models suck."

I couldn't help but needle him now that I knew everything would be alright. I felt untouchable, finally safe enough to throw all of Richard's barbs back in his face. The balance of power had shifted to me now, and both of us knew it.

"You know what happened," Richard all but *snarled*. "Tell me. *Now*. And don't play dumb."

I sighed theatrically. "I couldn't if I tried, my aesthetically-challenged friend. I'm afraid your friends are in custody by now—and mine are free."

Believe it or not, Thomas actually *reacted* to that. He opened his mouth to speak, but Richard smacked him and his lips slammed shut. "I don't suppose you'd tell me how that happened, Mud?"

His voice was velvet-soft again, and deceptively

calm. But I'd seen the anger beneath the surface and I could see it still, fighting to get free.

"I could," I said, yawning. "Don't feel like it. It was really clever, though."

"Really clever," repeated Richard. "Except you're all alone with two rather *incensed* armed men."

Right. I wasn't *completely* in the clear yet.

"Don't insult my intelligence by implying I didn't plan for that," I retorted, projecting a confidence I wished I felt. "You think I couldn't set up *two* ambushes? I didn't choose this place at random. The police are here, following an anonymous tip-off. They're searching nearby, but if, say, a gunshot were to go off . . . well, I daresay they'd hear. And they'd come in force. So I wouldn't recommend firing . . . or taking another step towards me, or I'll shout."

Richard, who'd raised his gun as if to strike me with it, stopped cold. But he didn't lower it. "That's assuming I believe your bluff."

"Sure. You don't trust me. That parked car over there with the seven antennae and the roof array is just a *convincing facsimile* of law enforcement."

Richard followed my finger back along the dock. There, further up the road and barely visible beneath a streetlight, was the unmistakable silhouette of a police car.

"The murder of a minor . . . " I shook my head. "They don't let you buy your way out of *that*."

Richard was twitching with rage, and I could see dark patches in his pale cheeks, even through the darkness.

"But as much as I'd love to put you behind bars, I'm afraid we're at a bit of an impasse."

"Yes," said Richard. "Since if you raise the alarm, I'll kill you, and if I try to kill you, you'll raise the alarm."

It was so matter-of-fact, the way he said that. It wasn't even a threat, just a cold assessment of the situation. My life held no value for Richard whatsoever.

Realizing this sobered me, even as it bit into my skin with the night chill. I *do* value human life, despite my attitude towards their possessions. Before Richard, I'd only met one other person who didn't.

And lucky me, I'd spent most of my life dealing with him. I had the tools and experience I needed—I'd built them over years of sharing a house with Lucas.

"It's a difficult situation," I admitted. "But there's an easy solution. We go our separate ways. I don't die, and you don't go to prison."

"And the moment we leave, you get the cops and they nab us before we make it three blocks. Don't insult me, *kid*—I'm smarter than that."

"I figured you'd say that, so I thought of a solution."

Richard narrowed his weasel eyes. He sensed a trap. "Which is . . . "

"You're familiar with the concept of incentives? A tool to nudge people towards courses of action they wouldn't otherwise take. As such, a financial incentive would *certainly* keep me from squealing. Once you feel safe, you wire me one . . . no, two million dollars."

He laughed, but the laughter was harsh now, rather than jovial. "Really fucking funny, kid."

"I'm *very* serious. You can't kill me, because the

noise will attract attention. You can't run, because I'll set the cops on your tail. You *definitely* can't stand here until sunrise. There's only one way out for you, and it'll cost you two million. The price of playing, we'll call it. I know your net worth, so don't pretend you can't afford it."

Not to toot my own horn, but it takes a special kind of person to extort a man who's holding you at gunpoint.

I saw the wheels in his head turning, but the gun in his hand didn't waver. He could've shot me dead. I could tell he wanted to. But in the end, self-preservation won out, combined with the realization that I couldn't force him to pay.

"Thomas, we're leaving," he said quietly, after shooting one last glance at the parked car. "It's a deal, you piece of shit. I'll leave an e-mail in my box when I get home."

I wanted to sag with relief, but I held my composure. "Pleasure doing business with you."

The two of us stood face to face in the shadow of the crane. For a moment, I thought he might actually snap. But he just turned and started walking back up the dock, with Thomas following behind like a lapdog.

I waited until they were about fifty paces away, then, "Richard."

He turned slowly, reluctantly.

"This time, we were out to fleece you. You're two million poorer, but you're none the worse for wear. Except we know your name, address, job, net worth, eye color . . . all sorts of things. You come looking for revenge, or if I don't get that two million within a few days, we'll come after you. And this time, the plan won't involve leaving you unharmed. But you have my word—don't fuck with me or mine, and I'll let you be."

I couldn't read his expression in the darkness, but I could see him squirm. Good. He'd taken me seriously.

"I trust I've made myself clear," I said. "You may go."

He hesitated, then motioned to Thomas. I watched their silhouettes shrink until they merged with the darkness, then waited a few minutes more until I heard an engine start. But I didn't allow myself to think I was safe. I carefully threaded my way through the dock's storage crates, taking an unfamiliar path in case one of them had stayed behind to ambush me. My ears were pricked for the sound of breathing or approaching footsteps, but I reached the other side without incident. Finally I could believe they'd really gone. Only then did I let my knees buckle in relief and sink onto the pavement.

I'd done it. In one masterstroke, I'd saved the entire CPC *and* potentially tripled the job's payoff. My body pumped with a mix of pride, elation, and exhaustion. For once, Lucas wasn't saying anything in my head, just clapping in the corner. In his place were my friends' smiling faces—Kira's good-natured grin, Z's reluctant approval, and Addie's . . . well . . .

I still hadn't figured out what she'd been thinking at the party. But maybe, just maybe, she'd be in the mood for a repeat. I looked once more for Richard and Thomas just in case, then trotted towards the police car, hoping they could help me home.

FOURTEEN

I N A FAIR AND JUST WORLD, RESCUING YOUR FRIENDS
from a gang of criminals, facing down their ring-
leader, then convincing two suspicious cops to call
a taxi, would cancel school somehow. Or *at least*
happen on a Friday.

No such luck.

I arrived bleary-eyed, work incomplete. I barely
listened as Mr. Richter lectured me on my lack of
responsibility. I was too busy wondering how my
friends were. I'd collapsed into bed the moment I'd
gotten home, and it's a miracle I'd made it to my
bed first. And since Richard had taken my phone, I
hadn't been able to call them today.

I managed a five-minute nap during Spanish, and woke feeling slightly better. By lunch, I was practically bouncing out of my chair. I was already halfway out the door when the bell rang.

This time, there was no verbal response when I knocked. Instead, the door swung open and, before I could protest that I hadn't given the countersign, Kira flung her arms around me. "He's here!"

"Jason!" exclaimed Z's voice from deeper in the room. "You're alive!"

"Never better," I said, smiling warmly. "Glad to see you're all okay."

"Well, Addie took a bullet to the chest, but—"

"I did *not*," said Addie, finally walking into view. "We've been calling . . . "

"Richard took my phone," I explained, disentangling myself from Kira and hugging Addie. "And then I got home really late and crashed."

Z frowned. "That gonna to be a problem?" He held out his arms and I hugged him too.

"What, the phone?" I actually hadn't considered that.

"He's got our names and messages."

" . . . Nah," I said. "I don't think he'll mess with us again. But that reminds me . . . "

Everyone wanted to know why I needed to access Richard's account again, but I evaded their questions. I wanted it to be a surprise. Eventually, Kira shrugged and went with it. I was shot through with anticipation, and every clatter of the keyboard was a hammer to my nerves. Just as before, there was one draft, with the heading, Fuck you, but I did it. I never want to see you again. The message was empty.

"The fuck does *this* mean?" wondered Kira, but I was already shoving her aside, logging into my own account, almost delirious with hope—

There. An e-mail from PayPal. I read the contents four times over and *still* couldn't believe he'd done it.

Z saw the e-mail over my shoulder and goggled.

And then, of course, I had to tell them everything. They listened appreciatively, gasped and applauded at all the right moments. Then I finished and asked,

"What happened on your end?" And everything came to an awkward, silent halt.

Kira and Addie sat down at that familiar table, around which we'd planned so many escapades. Z, seeing them, sat as well. I followed suit—I didn't know what was going on, but I *could* take a hint.

Kira began to speak, her tone far more serious than before. "Look, don't take this the wrong way. We're all super thrilled you're okay, and we don't wanna dump this on you, but we already talked it over a bunch, and none of us think it can wait."

"Here's what went down," said Z. "Right after you left, Richard told his groupies the real plan. They were gonna hold us at a new location in case you tried something funny, then kill us once you'd given him the money. We were all real mad at you for not seeing that coming, especially since *we* all did. We figured you *had*, and were saving your own ass."

I bristled indignantly. "What kind of person do you think I *am*?"

"But soon as we got there, the cops had us

surrounded. The thugs realized it was hopeless and gave up without a fight."

All according to plan, then. I made a mental checkmark in my personal scoresheet's "Victory" column.

But that didn't explain why everyone looked so *serious*.

"Fact," said Addie. "The three of us escaped a hopeless situation through police intervention."

"Fact," said Z. "You had police waiting at the docks to save you."

"Fact," said Kira. Jesus Christ, they'd rehearsed this. "None of us set up our rescue. You set up yours, stands to reason you set up ours too."

Back to Addie. "Fact. None of us *knew* we'd be rescued."

"Fact. As stated in the constitution of the Club for Perfect Cleanliness, no secrets relating to club business are to be kept between members." Z punctuated this final statement with a glare.

"Don't tell me you're actually mad about that."

I looked at their faces. "Alright, you're mad. I can tell you've all—"

"They were *this* close," said Addie, holding her thumb and forefinger a hair's width apart. "This close to shooting us dead. What if they'd just done it? Or taken us somewhere else, somewhere nobody was waiting for them. You couldn't have set up ambushes *everywhere*—"

"No," I admitted. "Before Kira and I went in, I called the NYPD posing as a repentant member of Richard's group. I told them the group was kidnapping and ransoming high school students, and gave them two locations, one eighty-four Eleventh Avenue, and South Street Seaport. Took some convincing, but they agreed to monitor the areas for a few hours. I'd already decided I'd use Pier Eleven if I had to—"

"When'd you decide that, exactly?" asked Z, suddenly looking at me intently.

"Oh, back when I was putting the original plan together . . . " I trailed off, realizing where this was going.

"So you thought Richard might come after me, *planned around it just in case*, and completely forgot to mention it. Unbe-fucking-lievable."

"Hold up." That was Kira, who'd been smoldering in silence from her seat. "We figured out that Richard abandoned his safe house as compromised. So why'd he take us there?"

I smiled. "Ah, *that* was the masterstroke. I knew they'd move you once I left—for all they knew, we'd already called the cops on that location, so they couldn't stay. One eighty-four Eleventh Avenue *had* been compromised, but as the people who'd compromised it were safely captured . . . and there wasn't any reason the police would be hanging around *there* . . . "

"They could've had another safe house," Addie pointed out softly. "They could've had dozens."

"Remember what I told you before I left?"

Addie wrinkled her brow, trying to remember. "About how I helped you become a better person? It was nice, but I don't see—"

"I said, exact words, that I'd had trouble coming out of my shell, see. My shell, see. Schell, see . . . "

Z saw it first. "Chelsea."

"Bingo." Despite the trial-like nature of the conversation, I couldn't help but feel a little pride. "I said there were *a hundred eighty-four* ways I could be doing something, and that I'd chosen the *Eleventh Avenue.*"

I saw the admiration dawn in all three as they figured it out, and I basked in it. *That* was more the reaction I'd expected.

"I primed him to think about the Chelsea safe house so it'd be the first secure location he thought of."

Kira blinked. "That definitely should *not* have worked."

"Why didn't you just tell us you had a plan?" asked Addie.

"To make your reactions real," I explained patiently. "You had to sell the lie, or Richard would've—"

Addie raised an eyebrow. "You didn't trust me to sell a lie?"

"That's not what I—"

"*Had to sell the lie,*" spat Z. "Dude, we were scared as hell. We thought we were all dead. You said this'd be safe, that Richard'd be a wimp. Nice job there, dude. That was the safest thing I've ever done."

I held up my hands in protest. "Kira found him. She didn't mention—"

"Oh, it's *my* fault now?" said Kira. "That you fucked up and didn't notice he was some secret underworld kingpin? Or maybe you *did* notice, and just didn't tell us because you had a *plan* if *shit went down?*"

She hadn't *started* calm, and her voice only got louder and angrier from there. Addie put a hand on her shoulder to quiet her. She shrugged it away angrily, but she *did* look a little more relaxed.

"I'm sure Jason didn't notice," said Addie.

"Wasn't *my* fault," snapped Kira.

"No," said Z, looking at me contemptuously. "It wasn't."

"I got us out alive—"

"You gambled with our lives," said Z firmly. "And you didn't tell us. You knew all that'd happen—"

"—I took the possibility into account—"

"—And just let it. So you had a plan, big deal. Maybe if you'd told us, we could've figured it out so we didn't need one at all."

Maybe if I reminded them of the payoff . . . "What about the two million dollars? Surely that was worth a little risk?"

Addie shook her head. "The money's not the point. You don't get it."

"What don't I get?" Of course the money was the point. We'd gone after Z instead of giving it back. Addie'd broken down at the thought of losing it. I'd *tripled* our payouts, and this was the thanks I got? Lucas's laughter was echoing in my head. *This is what happens when you trust people*, it was saying, and I set my teeth against it. "Do you want your share, or not?"

"Yeah, I want the cash," said Z. "I'll take the cash. But here's what you aren't getting. I'm *out.*

All of us are. I can't even trust you to tell me when I might get kidnapped? No wonder your plans keep screwing me over."

I opened my mouth to respond, but the words withered in my throat. Out? Like *out*, out? Of the *CPC*?

"I'm out too," said Addie. "I thought you'd betrayed us, back at the house. And *now* I know you didn't, but the fact that I suspected it . . . it showed me how far I trust you guys. And if I can't trust you, I . . . "

She trailed off awkwardly, but she didn't need to finish. "Thanks for helping my mom, though," she muttered.

Everything I'd worked towards was crumbling apart. I looked towards Kira, my stalwart bastion of support—

"Bro, you fucked up," she said, avoiding my eyes. "You know I'm all about this life, but not when—"

A full-body shudder rippled down her frame and she cut off abruptly.

You could've heard a raindrop fall. It was the biggest admission of weakness Kira had ever shown.

"Like, my family doesn't know about any of this shit," she said smoothly, like nothing had happened. "Doesn't even imagine it. And if I *died* . . . well. It'd fuck them up bad. You know that. And you put me up against freaks with guns. Not cool."

"*You* were excited to—"

"I *know*," she said forcefully, practically growling the words. "But—well, I'll just have to get my kicks another way."

I nodded dumbly, still reeling. My brain spun counterargument after counterargument, but my mouth wasn't cooperating. It knew the CPC was over. Why delay the inevitable?

"So, uh . . . meeting adjourned, I guess," said Z hesitantly. "It was a good run."

"Lotta fun," said Kira, getting up. "Later, bitches."

My failure tasted like bitter ashes in the back of my throat, and no amount of swallowing was getting rid of it.

Z was the first out. He picked up his backpack, nodded at me, and left. The door shut behind him.

Kira was next. She strode out with purpose, eyes fixed towards the door, unwilling to show her hesitance—if she had any. I wanted to think she did, but she would've thought it a weakness. And Kira doesn't show weakness.

And then there were two.

"Addie . . . " I croaked. My mouth was dry.

"Don't, please. I can't tell you." Her voice came fast, cutting me off before I could ask. Guess she'd figured out what I wanted to know, even if *I* hadn't.

On the smallest level, I wanted to know what she'd been thinking when she'd "kissed" me.

On a larger level, I wanted to know what she really thought of me.

And on the largest level of all, I wanted to uncover the secret in her heart, the one she'd built the rest of herself to hide. The one that I'd glimpsed in the taxi, but that ultimately remained hidden. Addie the Enigma.

So many questions . . . and no answers.

Her thin lips curved in a sad, bitter smile. "Bye, Jason," she said, and then she turned and walked out of the room, leaving me alone.

I stared at the door and breathed slowly. I'd come to rely on Kira and Z like my own arms, and I was feeling their loss like twin amputations. And Addie . . . well. Losing her didn't feel so great either.

But I wouldn't let this be the end. These past few days—winning big at the poker game, sneaking into a fortified house, staring Richard down with nothing but my wits—they'd made me feel *alive*. Being Jason Jorgensen, Normal Student, again would've killed me.

So I didn't go back, not yet. And I didn't leave Room 206.

I sat quietly, fingers steepled, and planned.